THE WARRIOR SONG OF KING GESAR

To Noah,
from Dad
Christmas 2001

THE WARRIOR SONG OF
✳ KING GESAR ✳

DOUGLAS J. PENICK,
Magyel Pomra Sayi Dakpo

WISDOM PUBLICATIONS • BOSTON

WISDOM PUBLICATIONS
361 Newbury Street
Boston, Massachusetts 02115
USA

Library of Congress Cataloging-in-Publication Data

Penick, Douglas J. 1944–
    The Warrior song of King Gesar / Douglas J. Penick.
        p.   cm.
    ISBN 0-86171-113-0 (alk. paper)
    1. Gesar (Legendary character)—Poetry.   2. Epic poetry,
Mongolian—Translations into English.   I. Title.
PL3748.G425P46   1996   96–20173
895'.41—dc20

0 86171 113 0

01   00   99   98   97
    6   5   4   3   2

Designed by: LJ·SAWLit

Cover art courtesy of Michael and Carolyn Rossip Malcolm collection, New York.

Typeset at Wisdom Publications using Adobe Garamond and Truesdell fonts.

Wisdom Publications' books are printed on acid-free paper and meet the guidelines for permanence
and durability of the Committee on Production Guidelines for
Book Longevity of the Council on Library Resources.

Printed in the United States of America.

CONTENTS

PUBLISHER'S ACKNOWLEDGMENT

The publisher gratefully acknowledges the generous help of the Hershey Family Foundation in sponsoring the production of this book.

ACKNOWLEDGMENTS

This book would not exist without the kindness, generosity, and commitment of many people. First amongst them is the late Vidyadhara, the Venerable Chögyam Trungpa Rinpoche, whose vivid inspiration is an unquenchable beacon of light. The teaching of His Holiness Orgyen Kusum Lingpa, the support of Sakyong Mipham Rinpoche, and the wide-ranging advice of the Venerable Tulku Thondup have also been of incomparable value.

The text was written at the request of Peter Lieberson for a chamber opera, *King Gesar*, commissioned by the Munich Biennale at the behest of Hans Werner Henze. A generous grant from the Witter Bynner Foundation For Poetry enabled the composition of this much longer rendition. Helen Boyer and Sarah Coleman have given continuing advice on the text and its presentation. Robin Kornman, Larry Mermelstein, and Sam Bercholz have also been unstinting with their knowledgeable assistance.

Timothy McNeill and Constance Miller of Wisdom Publications have been generously attentive in the preparation of this book for which Emily Bower has been a most patient and painstaking editor.

Douglas J. Penick,
Magyel Pomra Sayi Dakpo

FOREWORD

Douglas Penick has been a student of my father, the late Chögyam Trungpa Rinpoche, for many years, as well as a good friend of mine. I've appreciated his friendship, intelligence, and sense of humor a great deal during this time.

Some of the great attributes of Gesar of Ling that Douglas has brought to life in his book *The Warrior Song of King Gesar* are the energy and unpredictability for which Gesar of Ling has been and continues to be so loved and embraced by the Tibetan people through the centuries.

It becomes obvious that Gesar, and the epic of his life, represent more than a simple fable or historical documentation—but rather the life-force and energy of Tibet. Gesar of Ling means many things for the Tibetan people, and since his fame has now spread to the West, for humanity as a whole. He represents our dreams; our hopes of overcoming incredible odds; of being victorious and kind at once; of being vast and at the same time noticing small pebbles alongside the road.

I hope that the wisdom, imagination, and humor with which Douglas has conveyed both Gesar's story and the energy of his being will rouse unconditional confidence throughout the world.

May King Gesar's inspiration bring all humanity under the single flag of victory over war.

Sakyong Mipham Rinpoche
November 1995

INTRODUCTION

In nature you are the Vajra Manjushri.
In manifestation you are a divine king of the world.
In ancient times you were the knowledge-holder Padma Sambhava.
In the present you are Sengchen Norbu Dradultsal [Gesar].
In the future you will be Ridgen Rudrachakrin

—Mipham Namgyal[1]

Every now and then a spiritual or secular giant of unimaginable power appears on the world stage to bring order and harmony. About eight centuries ago, a glorious, miraculous man of amazing power took birth among the nomadic communities of eastern Tibet. He conquered many parts of that land and brought to it peace and the law of Buddhism. He was Gesar of Ling.[2]

Gesar was born[3] in the lineage of Ling in Dza Valley[4] in eastern Tibet. His father was Singlen Gyalpo[5] of Ling. His mother was Lhakar Drönma of Gog, popularly known as Gogza Lhamo or Gogmo. Singlen was the King of Ling, but being a person of gentle and feeble nature, he was losing his power to Todong, his ugly and cowardly—but short-tempered and loud—windbag brother. Because of the jealousy of Todong and Singlen's first wife, Gogmo and her infant son were forced to live at a distance from Singlen, and then were banished to the high grassy table-lands of the spectacularly beautiful Ma (*rMa*) Valley.

Gogmo named her son Chori. Chori grew up with his mother in a simple tent with no more than worn sheepskins to wear. He rode on a willow pole (*lChang dKar Ber rGa*) which, due to his enlightened power, moved faster than a horse. He used a herds-man's stone-throwing sling (*Aur rDo*), which miraculously became a powerful weapon. He was always under the protection and guidance of divine forces. His courage, brilliant wisdom and gift of divine power brought hope and joy to his parents and friends, but bitter suspicion and fear to the hearts of Todong, the contender for the throne of Ling, and his followers.

Before long, Chori obtained his mystic horse, Kyang Go Karkar, from the wild mountains of the north. At the age of thir-teen (or fifteen), against all expectations, Chori won his first vic-tory, the famous horse race of Ling. His trophy was the throne of Ling and the hand of Sechan Dugmo—the daughter of Kyalö Thampa Gyaltsen of Ga—as his consort, with abundant treasure. He proclaimed himself Sengchen Morbu Dradul, the Great Lion, Wish-fulfilling Jewel, Subduer of Foes. The youthful king assumed the golden throne of Ling. He was attired in warrior's armor and carried a divine bow, arrows, sword, spear, helmet and a shield, all adorned with resplendent jewels.

Gesar's main mission on earth was to defeat the enemies of his people's peace and to propagate and preserve the Dharma. Ling forces under the command of Gesar won eighteen major wars. Many of them were against foreign kingdoms or provincial tribes within Tibet. They include Lutsen Akhyung (of Kongpo?), the kingdom of Kurkar of Hor (Mongolia),[6] the kingdom of Jang Satham (Li-chiang in Yunan province), the kingdom of

Shingti (Mon), a kingdom of Tazig (Persia), a kingdom of Trugu (Turks) and Kangri Sheldzong (Ladakh) with its demonic supporters.[7] Those wars stirred up great turmoil not only in the camps of the foes but also for the Ling and their allies,[8] but it is believed that the wars brought long-lasting peace, joy, and Dharma to the lives of many.

Ling Chölha Phen of the Mugpo Dong lineage, mentioned in some literature on Gesar of Ling, is known as the famous forefather of Ling. Thirty-seven generations after Chölha Phen came Chöphen Nagpo. From his three sons—Lhayak Darkar, Changpar Trigyal and Dragyal Bumme—came the three major lineages of Ling leadership. They are the elder lineage (*Ch'e brGyud*), the middle lineage (*'Bring brGyud*), and the younger lineage (*Ch'ung brGyud*). Bumme's son was Thoklha Bum and his son was Chölha Bum. Chölha had three sons: Amye Rongsta Tragen, the eldest statesman of Ling in Gesar's time; Singlen Gyalpo, the father of Gesar and Gyaza (the half-brother of Gesar); and Mazhi Pönpo Todong.

Gesar raised hundreds of thousands of warrior men and women under the leadership of his legendary warrior commanders: the Seven Men of Supreme Warriorhood (*dPa' Yang Dag lDan Pa'i Mi bDun*), the Thirty Warrior Brothers (*Phu Nu Sum Chu*), the Eighty Champion Warriors (*dPa' Thul/brTul brGya Chu*) and the Eighteen Supreme Ladies (*Dvangs sMan bCho brGyad*). Among them, the most famous commanders were Gyatsa Zhalkar, Tsazhang Denma Changtra, Shenpa Meru, Amye Nanchung Yutag, Palha Michang Karpo, Dralha Tsegyal,[9] Atag Lhamo, and Jangtrug Yulha Thögyur.

Gesar was a manifestation of Guru Rinpoche. His chief commanders were also believed to be enlightened, appearing on earth solely to serve the world. Gesar constantly received teachings and prophecies from Guru Rinpoche and from many divinities and dakinis in pure visions, as from person to person. He also received teachings and transmissions from the great sage Amye Changchup Drekhol[10] of the Lang clan, and others.

Mahayana Buddhists believe that, in its true nature, the whole universe is oneness with the qualities of peace, openness, joy and enlightenment, which are buddha nature and the Buddha's qualities. However, we unenlightened beings—because of our entrapment in habitual webs of dualistic concepts rooted in grasping at "self" and self-afflicting negative emotions—live in the nightmarish life of conflict, pain and excitement. In order to serve an individual being, a community or the beings of an era, the power or quality of enlightened nature appears in various forms—such as beings, teachings, or things of nature—which are the symbols and sources of peace and joy. Therefore, any person or source that comes from and/or provides peace and joy for people—like the birth of Gesar—is the manifestation of the Buddha.

Buddhas sometimes appear in the forms, sounds, and actions of wrathful manifestations and expressions. These wrathful manifestations and actions come neither out of anger, attachment, and grasping at self, nor in order to harm or cause suffering to anyone. They come out of love and compassion, and they are powerful manifestations that destroy and eliminate the negative forces, the very sources of suffering.

Gesar's many wars are not expressions of anger, greed, or confusion, but of serving the needs of beings and the principle of truth. They were wars to bring the victory of right over wrong, peace over hostility, joy over suffering, and freedom over suppression through the action of compassion expressed in the form of war. The armies of Ling fought many wars, killed hundreds of thousands of people, and looted treasure after treasure through their skills in warriorship and their mystical power. But the sole goal was to eliminate the sources of suffering and suppression of people, and to spread and protect wealth, peace, freedom, and the Dharma for all, equally.

In the age of Gesar, the warriors fought according to the arts and ethics of heroes. Ling heroes would stand still before their opponents and listen to the songs-of-war (*sGrung gLu*) and await the poisoned and flaming arrow, spear, sword, or missile. True heroes of Ling and their warrior opponents hardly ever fought by hitting faster or by fleeing. They would cut off the enemies' weapons with their skill, strength of armor, or the help of divine protection—or they would fall victim. If they survived, with a war cry they they would sing the songs-of-war.

Ling warriors would always start their songs-of-war with the mantra of the Buddha of Compassion and an invocation of Guru Rinpoche or another deity. This was followed by the warrior introducing himself or herself, and a description of the field of battle. Then they would sing the reasons for the battle, the dangers of the weapons that they wielded, the crimes of their opponents, and the consequences that their enemies were about to face. Only at the end of such a monologue would they use weapons against their enemies. Among the Ling warriors there was hardly any event in which a warrior tried to run for his or her life, with the exception of Todong, who, a number of times, after provoking his enemies, ran away from the fighting and then disclosed Ling secrets in enemy captivity.

The wars of Gesar and his chief commanders not only brought peace and joy to Ling and to its enemies, but also ensured salvation for the fallen heroes of Ling and their opponents. For example, the two youthful commanders Pawo Ratna Bumthar and Agöd Senge

Drug of Ling realized that if they went to challenge the young Prince of Sog Litri,[11] they would lose their lives. But they also realized that because of their karmic connection with the prince, if they died in battle with him, their consciousness would be able to lead the prince's own mindstream into the Joyous Heaven (*dGa' lDan*). Other Ling warriors could kill the prince without any harm to themselves, but none could liberate his consciousness. So they knowingly volunteered to fight and die on the same field with the prince.

During Gesar's time, most of the Ling clans and their subjects inhabited the upper highlands of the Ma, Dza, and Dru valleys, around the sources of the great rivers of the world: Machu, the Yellow River (*Huang ho*); Dzachu, the Yalung River; and Druchu, the Yangtze River. Today these areas are occupied by the nomadic tribes of Golok and Lingtsang, and also by some of the Dege, Gapa, and Nangchen of eastern Tibet.

There are numerous literary works on the legend of Gesar known in Tibetan as Drung (*sGrung, epico*). They were written centuries after the time of Gesar. No literature about Ling written at the time of Gesar is known to have survived.[12] The Drung literature describes the wars of Ling in vivid detail, rendering the songs-of-war exchanged between the great warriors in the most rousing poetry. They also contain many profound teachings and prophecies.

Gesar was a real person and his victories were true events. The life of Gesar left vast physical landmarks, many hereditary successions, numerous artifacts, and profound historical contributions that prevail to this day. However, some scholars have doubted the very existence of Gesar. Gedun Chöphel (1905–1951) is one of them:[13]

The snow lion exists nowhere.
King Gesar is nothing but

A phenomenon that appears to fabricating minds,
Material proper only for poetic composition.

Gesar's influence on the spiritual and social life of his people is still felt in many parts of Tibet, Mongolia, Buryatsia, Kalmykia, and Tuva. In many parts of Kham and Amdo, and especially in Golok, people are still being entertained by the Drungpas, the Drung-singing specialists, who read and sing the stories and songs-of-war of Gesar for hours. Sometimes people pass whole nights listening to the heroic episodes of wars and the enchanting lyrics by bonfires, feeling as if they have become part of the warrior family of Ling.

For lay Tibetans, those Gesar epics remain a powerful source of inspiration, awakening inner courage in their hearts and knowledge of the greatness of their past. But serious students of the Dharma have generally shunned them as distractions from their studies and meditation.

Many of the Drung texts could be categorized as Mind Ter (*dGongs gTer*),[14] messages concealed in the enlightened nature of a realized mind and discovered through the power of enlightened wisdom. Among their discoverers are great adepts such as Do Khyentse (1800–1866), and celebrated scholars such as Mipham Namgyal (1846–1912).

However, most of the Drung texts are called Visionary Drung (*Babs sGrung*), written by gifted people such as Drungter Nyima Rangshar (twentieth century). Many of these Drung singers remembered the events of wars from their past lives as members of the Ling community under the leadership of Gesar.

Even today, Drung writers and Drung singers, like Drungpa Kelzang Tragpa, have special powers for recalling, retelling, and singing the endless epics of Gesar in beautiful poetry that flows spontaneously, as if the events were taking place right in front of them.

Also, a great number of people with gifts of language and imagination have written fictional Drung on the life of Gesar of Ling. Thus, it is not easy to present any information on the life of Gesar by separating fact from fiction. Nevertheless, I have attempted here to sift out some important points that are agreed upon by most of the sources that seem to be reliable.

Gesar was not only a defender of the Dharma; he also meditated in solitude for years and taught the Dharma, especially the nature of the mind, to a vast number of disciples. At Lhalung Yudo of Ma Valley, he sang his teachings to his uncle Amye Rongtsa Tragen, his minister Tsazhang Denma, and a huge assembly of people.[15]

The creator of our delusory world is our own mind.
But (in that mind), no beginning, middle, or end can be found.

The original nature (of mind), unmarked by any delusions,
Is called the primordial basis (*Thog Ma'i sPyi gZhi*).

From it arises the notion of grasping at an "I":
This is called the ignorance of the single self (*bDag Nyid gChig Pu*).

From it arises grasping at the five lights of wisdom as "other":
This is called the ignorance of duality (*Lhan Chig sKyes Pa*).

From it arises conceptual thinking and analyzing:
This is called the ignorance of discursive thoughts (*Kun Tu rTog Pa*).

From it arises the defilements and the sense consciousnesses

Together with the fifty-one mental events.

At that point you have become deluded
Into the three realms of samsara.

In the beginning, our mind does not come from anywhere,
But just bursts out due to adventitious conditions.

In the middle, our mind has no place to dwell,
But just holds itself up in samsara by mere attachment and clinging.

At the end,
Our mind has no place to go.

If we recognize these points,
We are liberated.

We cannot perceive the comings and goings (of our mind),
But due to the conditions of our karmic stream, comings and
    goings appear....

By asserting all sorts of labels
And by the force of our attachment to them,
As if we were binding ourselves with a rope
And then immediately killing ourselves,
Our delusions bind us
And cause us to wander to our death in samsara
With no chance of escape....

If we understand these, our own flaws,
We will realize our own mind as the Buddha....

As all thoughts are mere drawings on water,
By letting them vanish and dissolve without a trace,
Perfect the state of complete equanimity.

In India there are three teachings (on the nature of mind):

The great Middle Way, the Madhyamaka,
Shows the view that goes beyond the realm of conceptual thought
    and analysis.
This is the ground of the nature of our mind.

The great Sign, the Mahamudra,
Shows the way of meditating one-pointedly
And attaining the simplicity
Beyond the elaborations of the development and perfection
    stages.
Realizing the one-taste of samsara and nirvana,
Perfect the state of no-meditation.
This is the path of training (the nature of mind).

The Great Perfection, Mahasandi (*Dzogpa Chenpo*),
Perfects spontaneously the expanse of the intrinsic awareness
As the Dharmakaya, Sambhogakaya, and Nirmanakaya.
This is the attainment of the fruition (the nature of mind).

At the age of eighty-eight, Gesar summoned Tsazhing Denma, the only old warrior commander who was still alive, and the warrior princesses of the young generation with his beloved Ling subjects to Sengdrug Tagtse, his main palace in Ma Valley. After giving Dharma teachings, he declared that the time of his final departure had arrived. The next day many saw him flying away through the sky sitting on a shawl of light held up by four dakinis, and then he disappeared. Others saw him dissolving into a rainbow body, leaving the clothes that he was wearing but no mortal body behind.

According to Mipham[16] and some others, Gesar will reincarnate as Rudrachakrin, the twenty-fifth Rigden king of Shambhala, in that mystical hidden land of central Asia. It is also said that in A.D. 2424,[17] Rudrachakrin will conquer the dark forces and inaugurate the dawn of a new golden age of peace and joy on earth.

Tulku Thondup Rinpoche
Buddhayana, Massachusetts

Calling on the Power of Goodness in Our Hearts:
An Invocation to the
Imperial Drala, Gesar, King of Ling

✳

PART I

1

i

The white smoke of the juniper rises
Fragrant and dense from the burning coals,
Billowing into an empty shining sky,
A vast mirror-like expanse
Unclouded by the shadow of birth or fear of death.

There, descending on this perfumed bridge of smoke and longing,
Swirling and roaring in the smoke clouds, as in a gathering storm,
Surrounded by a host of mounted Drala and Werma warriors,
Whose golden armor and steel sword blades glitter like lightning,
Rides the great and ever-youthful conqueror
Gesar, King of Ling, Lord of the four kinds of warrior,
Destroyer of the four great demons who enslave men's minds.
He rules over the high snow mountains and the rolling plains.
He conquers fear, doubt, corruption and deceit in the hearts of men,
And is the great friend and protector of the life of all.

His reddish-brown face is implacable and his dark eyes fathomless.
His ferocious tiger smile is enticing.

His crystal helmet blazes like the sun.
His silver shield shines like the moon.
His chain-mail armor glitters like the stars.
He wears a tiger-skin quiver and his arrows are lightning itself.
His leopard-skin bow case holds the black bow of the north wind.
His sharp crystal sword is the invincible wisdom of spontaneous
    liberation.
With his right hand, he raises a terrifying whip that slashes
    through all deceptions,
And with his left, he raises a victorious banner the color of the dawn.
With saddle and bridle of pure white jade, he rides the miracle
    horse,
Kyang Go Karkar, who is the power of confidence, the wind of
    winds.

Gesar and his host of warriors gallop down the bridge of billowing
    smoke
Like a thunderstorm sweeping across a desert plain.
The thunder and roar of their charge overwhelm the fearful,
And their violent cries of KI and SO paralyze all cowardice.
Gesar comes like a wheel of iron rolling across the sky,
And the earth becomes still.

ii

Our earth is wounded.
Her oceans and lakes are sick;
Her rivers are like running sores;
The air is filled with subtle poisons.

And the oily smoke of countless hellish fires blackens the sun.
Day has become night.

Fish are born deformed; birds fall lifeless from the sky.
Forests and plains wither.
Animals running in futile search for shelter and food
Collapse and die.

Men and women, scattered from homeland, family, friends,
Wander desolate and uncertain, scorched by a toxic sun,
Prey to empty longings, strange diseases and sudden death.

Nor is night a cooling time of moonlit rest,
But a fearful flame-lit void
Of sirens, cries and murderous phantoms.
In this desert of frightened, blind uncertainty,
Some take refuge in the pursuit of power, of knowledge and
    technique;
Some become manipulators of illusion and deceit;
Some take refuge in realms of self-satisfied passion;
And some build up a golden wall of simple wealth.

Men have become robots and zombies
As they have made these hopes and fears
Their ruthless demonic lords.

If goodness and bravery still dwell in this world
As other than a flickering shadow on the edge of sleep,
If wisdom and harmony still dwell in this world
As other than a dream lost in an unopened book,
They are hidden in our heartbeat.

And it is from our hearts that we cry out.
We cry out and our voices are the single voice of this wounded
  earth.
Our cries are a great wind across the earth.
The juniper smoke rises on this wind,
And on this bridge of longing, as we sing of him,
Gesar himself, the ever-youthful Lion King descends
Surrounded by flags and pennants snapping in the wind
To forge the weapons that cut the life force of fear and doubt,
To subdue and destroy the demonic hordes,
And to establish the kingdom of freedom, confidence and joy
That dwells eternally in the hearts of all.

2

KI
From the shining purity of the cosmic mirror,
From the fiery bliss of wisdom and compassion inseparable,
From the thunderbolt confidence of warrior action,
The great being, the great hero Gesar, Destroyer of Demons,
Enters into this world, as a sword cuts through a paper wall.

His mother, Dzeden, is a dragon princess who has changed her
form to that of a young girl and has wandered far from her home
in the mists beneath the sea. Lonely and afraid, she works as a servant to Singlen, the aging King of Ling, who has taken her in and
given her food and shelter. One day while tending his horses in a
distant pasture, overcome by tiredness and sorrow, she falls asleep

and dreams. She dreams that a lord in silver armor, riding on a gray horse and escorted by six hundred gods who carry flags and umbrellas, descends to her along a golden rainbow. He approaches her and gives her a golden vase filled with nectar. He tells her that the future Lord of Ling and the conqueror of the demons of the eight directions has stared into this nectar and his form is imprinted in it. "Drink, and by this act a kingdom will be founded and all men will be liberated from their demonic lords." Dzeden obeys, and the lord, without another word, leaves as he came.

She returns home and falls ill. Singlen's jealous wife suspects that the girl is pregnant with her husband's child and abandons her. Dzeden feels she will die, but in the night she sees the tip of a white rainbow touch her head, and from the crown of her head appears a male child, white as a conch shell. He circles her three times and sings: "Mother, you will be rewarded for the kindness you have shown me," and he disappears into the sky. The next night a ray of red light touches her right shoulder and from there a flame-colored boy emerges. He sings the same words to her and likewise disappears. And then on the following night, a blue light touches her left shoulder, and in the same way a turquoise-colored boy emerges, speaks, and leaves. At dawn on the fourth day a ray of sunlight touches Dzeden's heart, and a young girl in the dress of a goddess emerges. She prostrates three times to her mother, says the same words, and returns to the sky.

Finally a few days later, while Dzeden feels sure she has gone mad, she hears a voice coming from her heart: "Mother, do not be afraid, but go look and see if it is time for me to be born." She thinks she may have been possessed by a demon, but asks what she should look for. "Go and see if your animals have just given birth; if a rain of white rice has fallen from the sky; if golden flowers bloom; and if the ground is covered with yellow, red, blue and black snow." Dzeden feels very foolish, but she goes outside and looks, and indeed all these strange things have taken place.

"Then, Mother, the time has come. Do not be afraid, for I will be born out of the crown of your head." And a few moments later, a white egg marked with three black spots pushes out of the top of Dzeden's head. She wraps it in a cloth and, a little while later, the shell breaks open and a strong ruddy boy steps out. Dzeden takes the little boy in her arms and rocks him lovingly.

Singlen's wife and Todong, Singlen's cowardly malicious brother, have seen the rain of white rice that shines in the sky and the golden flowers that have bloomed amid the yellow, red, blue and black snows, and they have seen that all the animals have at once given birth. Todong knows of the prophecy that these wonders can only mean: the future king of Ling has come. He fears that his own power and possessions will be reduced if such a thing takes place. Singlen's wife tells Todong that she suspects Dzeden is pregnant and may have given birth, and they go to investigate.

Todong, in order to look intimidating, puts on his bronze battle armor and helmet and goes on horseback to Dzeden's tent. As he draws close he hears the mother and child talking. "Daughter of demons, why have you given birth to a monster child in our lands? I should have had you killed when you first came here," he cries out, and he strides into the tent.

But when he sees the handsome, tiny boy standing in front of him, staring at him imperturbably with serious dark eyes, Todong knows in his heart that this is indeed the future Gesar. Despite his fear, Todong knows that if he does not kill him now, he will be subject to endless humiliations in the future. Brushing the screaming mother aside, he seizes the child and dashes his head against the tent post. But the boy only laughs. "Don't worry, Mother. It is not fated that this man can hurt me." Todong becomes more frightened and more furious. He ties the child's hands and feet with rags and buries him in a deep pit, which he covers over with thorns and a large flat rock. After Todong leaves, Dzeden weeps at the tomb of her child until she hears a voice from far beneath the earth. "Do not weep, Mother. Death does not exist for me. Death cannot interrupt my eternal vow to free men's minds." And indeed, when she wakes the next day, there is the little boy, walking back and forth, playing with a stick as if it were a sword.

Three days later, Todong becomes suddenly apprehensive. He wants to know if the child is truly dead, so he sends Singlen's wife to go look at the grave. But even from a distance, she can see that the child is playing with a little bow and arrow in front of the tent. She runs back to tell Todong. "It is as I feared. But if he cannot be killed by ordinary means, perhaps he can be destroyed by magic." So Todong mounts his horse and rides a half day to the cave of a hermit known throughout the land for his magical power. By means of lavish flattery and expensive gifts, the hermit is induced to perform the sorcery which will end the child's life.

The next morning, three large crows with feathers made of thin steel blades and beaks and talons of bronze circle Dzeden's tent. The child sees them and shoots them down with his arrows. But he knows the magician will try other spells, and so he goes to see him in his cave. The child arrives there completely naked. The magician is wearing long black robes, an apron made of human bones, and a tall hat decorated with bones carved as tiny skulls. In order to work his magic, he has set up a large altar in front of his cave and it is covered with the corpses of animals and snakes, with weapons, poisons and other fearful offerings. When the magician sees the naked shining child striding boldly toward him, he begins to sweat with fear. "What makes you so brave, you demon child? Is it possible you have never heard of me?" he calls out boldly. But even as he calls, he runs to hide behind his altar. "Oh yes," the child whispers, and his whisper is as audible as if the rocks and caves were whispering. "I know you. You have spent your life developing powers that help no one, so that you yourself can gain the admiration and wealth of others. Since I can neither admire nor pay you, how can I be afraid of you?" "Well then, we will have to see who is the more powerful," the magician challenges. "Invoke your gods and I will invoke mine. The loser shall die." "You have chosen your own fate," shouts the gleaming child with a voice like an avalanche, and he kicks over the magician's altar. The altar and all that is upon it turn into a huge boulder, which, as it rolls, forces the magician back into his cave and imprisons him there without hope of escape.

Then the child Gesar and his mother, taking with them their few possessions, go to a deserted region two weeks distant where they can live in safety. But it is a harsh and arid place, and as they walk there, Dzeden asks him how they will manage to survive, and what is the meaning of all that has happened so far. To comfort her, Gesar sings the song of his childhood:

Mother, I have never known the world to be impure,
So I have never had an enemy.
Mother, because there has never been an enemy,
My view is unmistaken.
Mother, I have always cherished others' happiness before my own,
So I am the child of illusion.
Mother, since I am the king of an illusory realm,
I am not anxious to accomplish anything,
So I have neither hopes nor fears.
Mother, as you can see, I am at peace.

I am your doubtless child;
This family inheritance is yours as well.

Things that frighten other people,
And things that entice those concerned with their own survival,
Look very different to my eyes,
For I see this world as the reflection in a sword blade
Which sings a beautiful song when it cuts through the sky.
Mother, look at this sword, our family heirloom,
And you will see as I do.

Mother, by your kindness, I have a good body,
Made in this realm from the four elements.
And because of your loving words,
I have the power of speech.
Without these, goodness cannot appear in this world.
Thanks to you this is so.
Even though it may appear strange, painful and frightening,
If the power of goodness is to show itself,
It must enter through this gate,
And thanks to you this will be so.
When you see things truly,
You will not be afraid.

Mother, as you remember,
When I was born, all your animals gave birth.
Here is what that meant:
The mare's foal is the child of confidence and wisdom
And will carry me through the many battles I must fight.
The calf of the yak and kid of the lamb
Show that by conquest this land will be abundant,

And the birth of the dog
Shows that I will never be taken unaware.

The golden flowers that bloomed
Are signs that this land will be inhabited by many wise ones.
The black snow shows victory over the demon of the North.
My sword shall sever his many heads.
The blue snow shows my victory over the demon of the East.
I will put my saddle on his neck and kill him.
The red and yellow snows show victory over demon empires
In the West and South.
Mother, there can be no doubt,
My work shall be complete.

The rainbows that touched your body
And the gods that came out of you
Show that our family and the power of wisdom,
The unfailing guidance of pure presence,
Will never be separate.
So, Mother, do not fear
That we will ever be without true friends.

Even Todong's evil deeds are happy omens.
When he buried me under thorns and earth,
It meant that I shall possess the ground and plant life where I lie.
The great stone he put on top of me
Means that my power is stable as a rock,
And the rags he used to tie me up
Mean that I shall soon wear royal robes.

My victory over the magician, his spells, and the beings he sent
    forth,

Show that there is no evil power in body, speech and mind
That can move me from accomplishing what I will.
So, Mother, do not fear;
Our seeming enemies are our real benefactors.

And even though our life seems now harsh and poor,
Sun, moon and starlight bless us with unfailing light.
We are sustained by rain and snow,
Nourished by wild cattle, the grass and the earth.
We live in a splendid place the gods themselves admire:
Gleaming snow mountains are our palace walls,
And this vast, green plain is our reception hall.
Mother, do not fear a life of poverty
When we are so well provided for.
Do not be blinded by slavery to conventional views:
When free of them, all riches are yours.
Gesar's heart is a crystal sword.
Because you kindly gave him this human form,
He enters the heart of all phenomena.
He is the life of all, the breath of all.
He is the light of light and the light in darkness.
He is the dance of the elements and the elements themselves.
He is the vividness of the senses and the senses themselves.
He is the spirit of guidance and the true law.
O Mother, do not be afraid of me.
Look in my eyes and see
The deathless realm that has never known despair.

Soon, Mother, this gleaming crystal razor sword
Shall be drawn and shine so bright
That even the blind shall see.

13

I shall utterly destroy
The dark dominion of the demon lords,
And my kingdom will be without boundary in time or space.
The mere thought of me will liberate all men from fear,
And the sight of me, who has never known hesitation,
Will fill the cowardly with terror,
And those who long for true freedom with joy.
O Mother, no matter what you may feel,
From the longing in your good heart,
You have given birth to this.

PART II

1

In the years he spends in the desert with his mother, Gesar grows into manhood. His body becomes tireless as the earth, his strength is as unflagging as the wind. He is lithe and fluid as a racing stream. His gaze is like the sun and his mind is like the sky. He rides his miracle horse, Kyang Go Karkar, born on the same day as he, and the two are as one being in their wild gallops across the plains. It seems that all of phenomena speak to him and are his playthings. His mother watches him grow with love and pride. But sometimes as she watches him racing on his horse, it seems to her that he is suddenly transformed into a whole army, or a great caravan, into an immense eagle or into a single lightning bolt. And sometimes when they sit quietly in the evening by the fire, he seems to disappear, and in his place there is a mountain, a small snake, an old ascetic, a mouse, a tiger. These things are puzzling, but somehow they make her smile as she passes the days, gathering roots, wild grain and berries, tending the hearth and making their life a contented one.

Then one morning, Gesar wakes to see Padma Sambhava, the lotus-born embodiment of spontaneous buddha activity, sitting before him in the eastern sky in his tent of dawn. In a voice as penetrating as a knife into his heart, the great guru speaks to him.

"Wake Gesar, Lion King of Ling. You are now a man and your dream-like life of peace here is at an end. You and I are one. I have brought the Buddha's teachings to the land of snows and taught the extraordinary path of meditation so that men can free themselves from mind-born slavery. It is for you to show the way that rests on the innate virtues of the human realm. It is for you to open the path of the four dignities. Join the ways of Heaven, Earth and Man, and bring into this world the kingdom of enlightenment, the deathless realm of true goodness and genuine dignity. Then, for as long as there is breath to tell of Gesar, King of Ling, all men and women will know that their life in this world is inseparable from the awareness and compassion in their hearts. This confidence will never leave them.

"To overwhelm the demon lords that dazzle men's minds and tether their bodies, you will enter inextricably onto the treacherous ground of this corrupt world. Guided by the pure presence of primordial wisdom, you will use worldly means. Your pure heart will fly straight through this world like an unswerving arrow, but due to the delusions of ordinary men, your acts will seem devious and strange. What look to them like guile, deception, illusion, seduction, lust, cruelty, confusion and slaughter are, in your hands, the magical weapons of liberation. You will show the path of the true warrior.

"Because you have never found a hairline of separation between yourself and your environment, you enter, at the heart, into the life of all. Thus you may change your form at will into whatever will serve the cause of goodness. You will show the path of the true king.

"Now is the time for you to act. Now is the time to enter this world. Singlen, King of Ling, whom many think is your father, has left his land to devote his life to spiritual practice. His venal brother, Todong, eyes the throne as a dog looks at a chop. Now is the time for you to establish your kingdom. Now is the time for you to become a king.

"Then, if your kingdom is to be secure and if the demon lords of the four directions are to end their merciless rule, you must obtain the sacred weapons concealed in the crystal cave of Magyel Pomra. You alone can open the command seal that hides them. Now is the time to do so.

"Then, if your kingdom is to be wholesome, you must seize the treasury of the Buddha's sutra teachings, which overcome the sufferings of mind, and the medicines which can bring relief from the body's troubles. These have been horded by Tirthika priests of great power who use them only for their own perpetuation. Now is the time to give them freely. All this must be done before the demonic kingdoms can be conquered, and the wisdom of the warrior path restored.

"Now that you are fully awake to what you must do, it is time for you to act without delay."

So saying, the great guru rises up on a bridge of blazing sunlight and disappears into the sky. That same morning, Gesar and his mother set out for Ling.

2

While they ride homeward, Gesar devises a scheme to trick Todong into making him king. He knows that for many years, Todong has been accustomed to divining messages in the cawing of the ravens which fly around his house. And so, in the middle of the night, when they are still two days away from Ling, Gesar transforms himself into a raven and flies to the window of the room where Todong sleeps. He wakes Todong from his stupor and cries out: "Hail Todong, future King of Ling. I come from the realm of the gods to help you. Tell the people of Ling that Singlen has died on his pilgrimage and that a successor must be found or Ling will fall. Tell the wealthy miser Thampa Gyaltsen that he must make the new king his heir, and that he must give his daughter, Sechan Dugmo, who is so beautiful and proud, in marriage to the new king. Tell one and all that the new King of Ling will recover a great treasury concealed in Mount Magyel Pomra." "But how, how shall I become that one?" sputters Todong who is now fully awake. "Tell all that by the order of the Buddha himself, there will be a horse race," the raven replied, "from which no one, rich or poor, young or old, shall be excluded, and the winner, the greatest horseman of the land, shall be Ling's king, Sechan Dugmo's husband, Thampa Gyaltsen's heir, and the sole possessor of Magyel Pomra's fabled treasure." "And, truly, I will win this race?" Todong is so excited that he can scarcely believe his ears. "Todong, choose your very best horse and do not doubt that the gods will make you victorious. You will be the victor, do not doubt it." And with that the raven flies off.

Todong is so overjoyed that he wakes his wife and tells her what he has just been told. But she, who knows her husband all too well, is ever doubtful of his plans. "You are being led astray by greed and lust. You are drunk and a bird is a bird. If you go ahead with this, you'll regret it." But Todong has seen himself king, with a new young wife and fabulous wealth, and he is not to be dissuaded. Next day, he summons the chiefs of the ten- thousand villages and tells them of the god's command. The race is set for three days hence, and all agree to bestow on the winner the prizes that Todong's raven has decreed.

The race takes place in a broad valley some five miles long. At the far end, beneath a yellow canopy, is a golden throne which marks the finish line. There wait all the noble wives and elders with Thampa Gyaltsen and his daughter, both dressed in gold brocade, and she with turquoise, coral and pearls braided into her hair. At the other end of the valley are massed the great riders of Ling in furs and silks astride their swiftest horses. The horses' tails and manes are oiled and braided with blue and red ribbons. Tinkling bells hang from their necks and their saddles are covered with beautiful carpets. All in all, the steeds seem as proud and vain as their riders, as if they too could become the ruler of Ling.

More splendid than all the others is old Todong. His robe is dark blue silk with a turquoise border and gold piping. His blue-black horse has a fine black mane and tail and carries a lizard-skin saddle ornamented with arabesques of gold and silver. Todong looks hungrily down the valley at the small form of Sechan Dugmo, who glows like a goddess in the sunlight. He feels utterly confident of victory until he sees, coming from far off, a scrawny nag, for so Kyang Go Karkar has made himself appear, loping towards them with the scruffy boy he once knew as Dzeden's son, riding bareback. At that moment he feels a twinge of fear and thinks that perhaps his nagging wife was in the right. But his fear is dispelled as a fresh breeze blows across his face, and he jeers at the unkempt rider. "Ho, you look like a goat on a donkey, you wretched son of Dzeden. Do you really think you will be allowed to ride here?"

Gesar is silent amidst the general laughter. But the elder who is to start the race calls out: "It is the rule that no rider can be excluded from this race." And with that everyone is quiet and they ride their horses up to the starting line. Horses, snorting, stamp and prance, and riders tighten up on their reins and adjust their stirrups. They wait tensely for the signal to begin as they jostle against each other, jockeying for the best position. But suddenly, the red banner is raised and the race is on. To the cries and shouts of their riders, a thousand horses' hooves shake the earth, and behind them a great tan cloud of dust swirls slowly into the sky.

Gesar's heart is cool and pulsing like a highland spring, and he holds tightly to Kyang Go Karkar's reins. He does not move. Even as the dust cloud far ahead rises higher and higher and all that can be seen of the racing horses are the sparks from their hooves, even as his heart beats, he feels a calm detachment as if he were an eagle watching from the sky. And the sight of all these brave men and noble steeds striving their utmost in the midday sun fills him with profound joy.

Kyang Go Karkar turns to look at him. "Are you having second thoughts?" he snorts. "Are you longing for our solitary rides across the plains?" Gesar smiles, shakes his head, but does not let go of the reins. "Such courage, such gallantry, such strength." He is filled with joy as he watches the host of warriors, "Ah, this world is truly good. What I will accomplish already is." The miracle horse shifts his weight, and Gesar's body and mind become one thing, one intention, one wish. He digs his heels into the flanks of the miracle horse, and with a great fearless leap, they rise into the sky. They fly through the sky as if on an invisible highway, and they land, racing amid the pack of riders, a third of the way down the valley.

Gesar is engulfed in a maelstrom of dust amid the sweating men and beasts. Riders slash their whips, their horses strain—lips flecked with foam, glazed eyes rolling madly. Suddenly it is as if there is no goal and no end; there is only this wild, raging tear across the earth, which has caught them all and hurls them forward. And Gesar feels a piercing and intimate sadness that this is indeed the way of men. And even as he feels weighted down with sorrow, he feels himself caught up in the same race. His mission of kingship, dominion, wealth, power, love, admiration, is this truly any different from that of the maddest of the racers in the whirling throng? Wherever he looks, he can see no difference. He spurs Kyang Go Karkar once again, and again, with one great leap, he is at the head of the charge with only Todong by his side.

Gesar laughs when he sees Todong's horrified surprise, and he whispers to his wonder horse, "Sweet little nag that in two bounds has overtaken the glory of Tibet, lash your hooves out at Todong and his steed and send them crashing to earth." And with that, Kyang Go Karkar pulls a little ahead of the old man and his handsome blue-black horse, and with a mighty kick into the trailing horse's flank sends horse and rider scattering to the ground. "Ah, why have you done this to me?" Todong cries out after him, and Gesar, looking over his shoulder, calls back: "O Uncle, I only mean to guard my treasure from those who would steal it from me, and your handsome blue-black steed got in the way." A final time, Gesar urges his wonder horse to make a mighty leap, and in one enormous bound, he crosses the finish line before the empty throne, while all the riders of Tibet are still a mile away.

And so, suddenly, Gesar is there before the throne, sitting on his miraculous horse who is nibbling peacefully at a clump of grass. He laughs and looks around him at the assembly of elders, noble ladies, at Thampa Gyaltsen in his gold brocade and at Sechan Dugmo in her turquoise, coral and pearls. And they are all staring at him in shock, for even if he is the victor, he is still merely a dirty wild youth in a worn sheepskin coat who has won the Kingdom of Ling on the back of an underfed nag. Gesar slides off the horse and quickly, before anyone can think to object, sits up on the throne. He knows it must be a strange sight, a rough urchin on a golden throne, but to him it seems fitting. And as he looks back at all those faces that are now turned upwards toward him, he can read in their eyes their innermost thoughts. Some are frightened; some suspect black magic; some are amused; some are already thinking of how they may curry favor with him; and some think of the prophecy that says that such a king will lead his people to unequalled prosperity. Thampa Gyaltsen is ready to overcome his misgivings, since regardless of how this boy may look, this boy is indeed the king of Ling, and even if he does not come to much, it will reflect credit on Thampa Gyaltsen's family. Sechan Dugmo, who out of her great pride has already rejected scores of better-looking suitors, is thinking of how she can find a way to reject him as well.

The sky is cloudless and dark blue, and the sun blazes brilliant and hot. It is a perfect day. Then all the riders of Ling come cantering up, laughing and cheering, though some are still teasing a bruised and dusty Todong in their midst; and when they reach the line before the throne they stop and bow.

In that exact moment, Gesar assumes his true form. His golden helmet flashes rays of light, while its white pennants flutter in the sky. His shield and armor seem to glow with their own radiance. His weapons are frightening. His smile is affectionate, but his gaze cuts through all deception. His voice is like a crack of thunder:

SO
Noble lords and ladies, brave warriors,
Know me as I am, the one who has been foretold.
It has been written in prophecies, and you know it in your hearts:
I am Gesar, King of Ling,
Who brings prosperity, dignity and joy,
Who destroys cowardice, delusion and slavery.

I am Gesar, Lion King of Ling,
The great conqueror and the great healer.
I am the light of your darkness,
The food of your hunger, and the scourge of your corruption.
I hold the sword of truth in one hand,
And the medicine of peace in the other.
The time of my kingdom is now.

Whether you doubt this or not, it is so.
Whether you fear this or not, it is so.
Whether you rejoice in this or not, it is so.
Whether or not you would like to return
To the petty schemes of private life,
It is so.

We are one in this kingdom.
We are one in dignity.
We are one in courage.
We are one in battle.
We are one in gentleness.
We are one in splendor.
We are one in delight.
We are the promise of this world,
And we are the glory of this world.
From today onward, I have entered your hearts.

The kingdom is won
When you ride without hope or fear
On the power of the great wind of winds,
Which causes the hearts of the unworthy to shake and cling,
Which is the confidence in the heart of the stainless warrior.
My great horse, Kyang Go Karkar,

Is this miraculous wind of winds,
The spontaneous power of the uncontrived.
Learn this, noble warriors and ladies,
And the kingdom of authentic presence
Will expand without limit.

This harsh and splendid land
With snow-covered rock mountains, cold crystal streams,
Deep forests of cypress, juniper and ash,
Where deer, snow leopards and downy rabbits dwell,
Valleys of soft grass where yaks and horses graze,
Vast skies of peace with blazing sun and dark wild storms,
The home of eagles, ravens, doves, owls,
With velvet nights of distant stars
And shadows of a pale moon,
Is as much my body as what you see before you here.
I cannot be separated from this or from you.
Our many hearts have only a single beat.

Now, so that our world shall prosper and increase,
I take this proud, disdainful lady as my wife.
I take Sechan Dugmo as a jewel into my heart.
When I look at her, I know that joy is truly without limit.
She is bliss itself and the banner of victory,
She is the well-being of our kingdom.
My life is in her gentle hands.
She is the golden garuda whose plumage outshines all others,
Who will sing her melodious song, nesting in the tree of my life.

With this, Gesar steps down from his throne and looks for a
long time at Sechan Dugmo. She does not know whether she is

completely terrified or strangely overjoyed. When Gesar suddenly unsheathes his sword, she feels she is going to faint. It is like a flash of lightning in broad daylight. And with his blade, Gesar cuts a vein in his palm. In a voice like a hurricane, he proclaims to the ten directions: "Now the root of world aggression is cut through, and the blessings of the Imperial Rigdens flow." With her red lips, Sechan Dugmo draws the blood out, drinks, and thereby becomes one with the father and mother lineage of Dralas. Gesar shouts out again: "A LA LA CA CA HE HE HO." She raises her head to look at him and laughs aloud and weeps for joy. The true kingdom becomes genuine in this moment, and Gesar himself, complete.

In this way, Gesar becomes king of Ling, and Sechan Dugmo becomes his wife and queen, and their subjects experience the dignity, gentleness and kindness of their kingdom. The celebrations and feasts of the people of Ling continue for three months. Gesar takes up residence in Singlen's palace, sets the affairs of his kingdom in order, and retires from public life for a time to meditate.

3

Early one morning when the sun has just risen over the mountain peaks and the full moon still floats in the sky, Gesar looks out from his window and sees his sister, the goddess Manene, coming toward him on an opaline rainbow. Her skin is the color of pearl, and she rides a white lion and leads a buffalo behind her; in one hand she holds a bow and in the other a mirror.

"Gesar, I am the wisdom that is forever yours and the guidance that will never fail. The sun, the moon, the planets and the stars are in a rare auspicious conjunction. The time has come for you to gather the warriors of Ling and lead them to Mount Magyel

Pomra. There, take the treasures that are held for you alone. The secret cavern will open to you. But be on your guard when you take the treasure back to Ling, for earthly demons will want to keep it from you and will harass you on the way. If you are careful, you will succeed, and the weapons and treasure needed for all your later battles will be yours."

So Gesar assembles all the warriors of Ling and they set out on the day of the full moon. After two days' ride, when they reach the foot of the great black mountain, Magyel Pomra, they pitch a vast array of white tents with silk pennants and sit before them on leopard rugs. All but Gesar are intimidated, despite themselves, by the high wall of cold somber rock that faces them.

Gesar sits motionless amidst his puzzled and restless warriors for more than a day. Through the night and the day, his heart throbs like a torch in the wind and his eyes bulge as he stares at the face of the black rock mountain range, which now seems to seethe with veins of burning lava. In the late afternoon, he begins to sing:

> Warriors of Ling, do not struggle.
> Light and awareness are indivisible.
> Just look into the mirror of the self-existing mind.
> See things just as they are.
>
> Because awareness and phenomena have never separated,
> The treasury of Magyel Pomra opens to me.
> This black rock mountain is the nature of space.
> This black rock mountain is a mansion of light.
> This black rock mountain is the gift of awareness,
> Marked only with the name of Magyel Pomra.
> Seeing it is the experience of compassion.

Because awareness and mind have never separated,
The treasury of Magyel Pomra is now open to me.

On the side of the mountain is a great gleaming crystal vase.
So rejoice, you peerless warriors.
In the vase is a golden lake of deathless *amrita.*
Let us drink, my thirsty friends.
Let us plunge into the honey-like waters of this golden sea.
Warriors, let us claim our birthright on the spot.
Leap. There is nothing to overcome.

And with a single bound, Gesar leaps up the side of the mountain to a protrusion that seems to have the shape of an immovable crystal vase. With a phurba grasped in his right hand, he makes the mark of cutting through on the crystal vase, and then shouts in a voice of thunder: "Here are the treasures hidden by Padma Sambhava. They are guarded by the twelve goddesses of the earth. I, Gesar, King of Ling, am their true owner. According to Manene's bidding, I am here to claim them." He knocks on the crystal wall with a golden dorje, and then he disappears as he steps through the sheer wall of rock. Stunned, his men follow him as quickly as they can. When they reach the ledge where they saw Gesar vanish, some see a thin glowing seam on the face of the mountain, some see a crack in the rock face itself, and some see simply a dull black wall.

But Gesar calls out again, the rock opens, and all the warriors of Ling pass into the mountain. They enter a huge crystal cavern suffused with a light as intense as the sun, the color of the autumn moon, and dense with sweet heavy incense. They are overwhelmed, oppressed, and feel engulfed. But as they begin to relax, they come to their senses. At the center of the crystal hall there is a great golden throne, and on the seat of that throne, the jeweled mandala of the world. At the center of the mandala is a glowing diamond vase overflowing with deathless *amrita*, and around it, long-life pills and threads. Around the walls are heaps of gold and silver armor, bows and arrows tipped with meteoric iron, swords with silver, gold and crystal blades. Awe gives way to delight as the warriors realize they are the possessors of this great treasure.

Gesar explains that the meaning of the mandala on the throne is that primordial awareness is deathless, and its movement is the wisdom and life force which pervades human life. Gesar then guides his men as they remove the contents of the miraculous cavern, which include, most importantly, a crystal helmet, a dorje of meteoric iron, a celestial sword, ninety-eight arrows with turquoise feathers, a great bow made of antelope horn, a jewelled whip and a turquoise spear called The Conqueror of the Three Worlds.

But as they are removing the long-life arrows of the people of Ling, a cloud of black wind knocks the arrows to the ground. They are aghast at this evil omen, but Gesar throws the iron dorje into the heart of the cloud and it disperses. Later, when they are back at the camp, they are attacked by a musk deer with a strange fantastic gait, a boar that lives on corpses, and a demented monkey. The first is shot by one of the warriors, and the other two are killed by kicks from the wonder steed, Kyang Go Karkar. Despite these strange events, Gesar and his army return joyfully to Ling.

When they have returned, Gesar sees that his warriors still feel some disquiet at the attacks they were subjected to and that their minds are clouded with a tinge of ominous fear. So, as they are feasting to celebrate obtaining the treasure, Gesar tells Sechan Dugmo what has happened and asks her to interpret these portents for the people of Ling. Inspired by Gesar's request, she sings this song:

> All-victorious Lion Lord,
> Great warriors of Ling, decisive and brave,
> You have made this land powerful and wealthy as never before.
> You threaten the demon tyrants as no one ever has.
> Demons are on guard and do not rest.
> They do not easily surrender their power over us.
> What took place today are not omens of defeat,
> But show the way to victory.
>
> The *amrita* and long-life pills and knots
> Mean victory over death and long life for this kingdom.
> When the black wind knocked over the long-life arrows,
> It means that the appearance of the kingdom will be interrupted.
> When the Great Lord dispelled the evil wind,
> It means that any interruption is merely a temporary illusion.
> When you were attacked by a deer, a boar and a monkey,
> It means that you are still afflicted by fears, ignorance and grasping.
> When the deer was killed by an arrow,
> It means that your warriorship will defeat fear.
> When Kyang Go Karkar slew the boar and monkey,
> It means that the authentic power of Windhorse
> Will destroy ignorance and greed.
> This being so, O mighty lords,
> Celebrate with a joyful mind.
> Let nothing distract you from joy.

Gesar is pleased and applauds Sechan Dugmo's wise words, and the people of Ling are happy and rejoice. A golden rain showers down and turquoise flowers bloom in all the meadows of Ling.

4

Once again, while Gesar is alone and at ease in his shrine room, the image of his sister, the conch-colored goddess Manene, comes to him across a silver rainbow bridge and speaks tenderly to him.

Your mind is free from obstacle and occupation
And courses, without moving, in the open sky.
Greetings beloved brother, lion-like friend of man.
You shine like the sun in the center of space,
And your kingdom basks contentedly in that protecting light.
How delightful it is to dwell here.

But, dear brother, beyond the borders of Ling,
There are lands where the virtues of the human realm
Are clouded by delusions of many kinds.
Oh, my brother, you must enter these dark realms
Even as the sun passes into a black storm and burns it away.
Otherwise, however happy your people may be,
They will always live on the border of fear.
If the sanity of your kingdom is to be without limit,
You must first demolish the stronghold of theism,
The realm of the Tirthikas, the realm of a dark god and of blood
    sacrifice.
Believing in the strength of goodness is the power of a god,
The people have been robbed of their own intrinsic strength,
Their dignity is stolen and placed in the hands of others.

The priests have accumulated a great store of precious medicines
And a great library of the Buddha's words.

But they hoard these very things that bring ease and freedom to
this life.

You must go there: destroy the Tirthika stronghold.
Return the god to his own realm and release his followers from slavery.
You must kill the high priest Lungjag Nagpo,
And free his daughter, who is a secret embodiment of mercy.
Then you must bring the teachings and medicines back to Ling.
This will assure all your future conquests.

Gesar sees that this is so and his heart flutters suddenly like that
of a small bird caught in a net. He smiles at his sister even as he
knows the cruelty of the painful world he will enter, and he bows
to her. Then, Manene dissolves into the sky across a silver rainbow.

5

Gesar then assembles the people of Ling, tells them what he must
do and that he must accomplish this deed alone and unaided. So,
despite the misgivings of his family and troops, he sets out on his
horse, Kyang Go Karkar for the Tirthika realm. His mother, his
wife, his fellow warriors and all the people of Ling accompany
him to the border and weep when he leaves the lands of Ling.

i

When he is out of sight, Gesar spurs Kyang Go Karkar, and they
fly through the air to a mountain-top deep within the realm of
the Tirthikas. Gesar finds a crystal cavern, called the Luminous

Sunlit Cave, where, with his horse alone attending him, he meditates for two months, according to the cycles of Vajra Kilaya and Four-Armed Mahakala.

The deity of the Tirthikas, moved by curiosity, annoyance, amusement and pride, appears before Gesar in his cave. His form is vibrant and immense, his body is covered with white ash, and his shiny black hair streams wildly like the king of rivers. He is naked except for a necklace of skulls and he is accompanied by thousands of menacing trickster demons playing hand drums and cymbals. He is the miraculous nature of consciousness itself. His laughter is bliss, his speech is light, and his dance is utterly mesmerizing. His effortless power is intoxicating.

Gesar's eyes are dazzled, his ears are deafened, his skin tingles, and his senses are overwhelmed, but his heart is still. Then, as if his arm had its own will, he suddenly draws his crystal sword. The sharp tip of Gesar's sword touches the sky and quivers there, and Gesar is filled with fierce joy. At the very point where sky and sword-tip meet appears a black dot, rich and splendid, with all the qualities of the blood, milk and ink of the Rigdens—dense and perfumed as a summer night with all the good qualities of the human realm. In the clear and shining sky, this black dot of relative truth, freed of conceptions, destroys all belief in an independently existing absolute. The heart of the god is pierced, and as Gesar's sword tip quivers, the dot forms an iron ring.

Gesar, King of Ling, feels in that moment the power of every sword that was ever drawn, of all the arrows ever shot, of each scepter ever raised up, and of every crown that was ever worn. The strength of every command that was ever given, and every law that was ever proclaimed flows in his veins. His body of flesh, blood and bone is itself the razor edge of longing of the ancestral sovereign. He stands and his body becomes the tent pole of the world; his feet cover all ground and the pennants of his helmet fly above the vault of the sky.

The form of the god pales and he returns to his own realm.

ii

Gesar calls to the miracle horse, Kyang Go Karkar, and together they fly to the center of a dense forest where an immense black serpent, who stretches taller than the walls of a great city, lives in an enormous sandalwood tree. This serpent is the living secret heart of Lungjag Nagpo, and is the embodiment of intimidation, venomous rapacity and terror. Gesar calls out to the serpent, and it emerges swaying and hissing, emitting the rotting smell of the charnel ground. It uncoils and towers over him, almost blotting out the sun. He shoots a single arrow into the serpent's forehead, and the creature crashes to the ground. Gesar cuts off its luminous horns and removes its eyes, whose pupils are made of iron, and he cuts out its blazing heart.

Then Gesar and his horse fly down to the vast dark cavern far under the earth, where dwells an immense bronze tortoise, the embodiment of the hidden and sustaining power that the hopes and fears of the disciples have brought into being. He hurls a phurba made of meteoric iron between its eyes, crushing the metallic skull of the monster. The bronze body is pulverized as the cave collapses down upon it. All that remains is a lightning-flashing jewel from the center of the tortoise's brain.

Gesar is exultant and, mounted on Kyang Go Karkar, in a swirl of rainbow light, flies to the summit of the sky. Raising his sword so that its reflections sparkle like stars in daylight, he cries:

Rigden Fathers, ancestral sovereigns,
Lineage of Sakyongs, single blazing sun of the world,
You are the wisdom, understanding, nourishment and comfort of
  the earth.

There is no atom of my being that is other than your
  confidence.
Kulika Kings of Shambhala, you, the summit of
  dignity,
As a moment in your vast imperial mind,
I establish the kingdom of enlightenment,
The birthright of all who live in the human realm.

KI KI SO SO

iii

On this very same day, many evil omens appear at the fortress of
the Tirthikas. Blood oozes from the neck of the golden vase that
holds the holy water on their shrine; a sudden wind shreds a cur-
tain made from human skin that hangs before their sanctuary;
and the bottom of the huge pot in which their tea is brewed shatters. Padma Chotso, Lungjag Nagpo's daughter, dreams that the
fortress has been burned to ash and all its occupants killed, so
that nothing is left except embers and dried blood, which wild
beasts lick from the rubble. A pervasive anxiety enters the hearts
of the Tirthikas, and Lungjag Nagpo decides that they must perform divinations and prepare themselves with arms and with the
magical powers of their prayers.

So that he may confuse their empty habits of mind, Gesar appears to the Tirthikas as the messenger of their god, a handsome shining eight-year-old boy, dressed in silk and draped in jewels, riding down to them on the great king of birds. "Your fears are groundless," he tells them. "These omens presage victories over your enemies. The skins of their bodies and the blood of their flesh will adorn your shrine. Your enemies will have nothing to support them and their strength shall spill out and be dispersed into the soil." The Tirthikas are most relieved and drop their guard a bit.

Several days later Gesar appears to them again, this time as the wise and dignified minister of their god. He wears copper-colored armor and rides on the back of a nine-headed elephant caparisoned with human skins. He prophesies that soon they will be attacked by warriors from Tibet, but if they remove all the bales of medicine and pile them around the four walls of their fortress and close all the gates, they will surely be victorious. Though the strategy seems strange to some, they do not hesitate to obey a god's command.

Finally, Gesar in his true form appears to Padma Chotso in her room. Although she is at first alarmed, the melodious sound of his voice puts her at ease:

Fear not, dear friend,
Though you have been born in the alien darkness
Of a cruel and deluded realm,
You have shown unfailing kindness to these misguided men.
Truly, only the fragrance of your compassion
Dispels the stench of carnage here.
Truly, only the delicacy of your courage

Is without the bravado of fear and self-interest.
Truly, only the clarity of your gentleness
Gives any light amid blood sacrifices.
Knowing the true and just fate of your race,
You still bless them with your gentleness.

O Princess, you are the truest warrior,
A crown jewel of the Drala Mother lineage,
And my heart melts on seeing your noble face.
Your long endurance makes all warriors humble.

Now the time of your painful struggle
Has reached its appointed end.
Tomorrow I will bring you to Shining Crystal Cave.
There you will put into practice all you have yearned for.
You are the delicate lotus who will come to full bloom
On the clear lake of the Buddha's path.
Tomorrow I will take you to your heart's home.

Although Padma Chotso grieves for her father's impending death, when she hears Gesar's words, she feels that a great burden has been lifted from her, as if she is in sight of home after a long and hard journey. Then, before her eyes, Kyang Go Karkar magically transforms himself into a small crystal dorje, which Gesar gives to her. "When the time comes, this will bring you to me." And with that Gesar disappears.

iv

Now begins the final destruction of the Tirthikas. The medicines have been piled high at the walls; the gates have been sealed, and

Lungjag Nagpo and his adherents wait within.

Gesar then emanates four identical warriors. From his body comes a warrior just like himself, but carrying a standard marked with a tiger, to stand at the Tirthika citadel's eastern gate. From his speech comes a warrior whose standard is marked with a lion to stand at the northern gate. From his mind comes a warrior whose standard is marked with a garuda, to stand at the western gate. And from his actions a warrior whose standard is marked with a dragon, takes his stand at the southern gate.

These warriors, the inseparable body, speech, mind and action of the great Drala Lord, Gesar of Ling, chant in unison:

LU TA LA LA. A LA LA LA. TA LA LA.

Rigden Fathers, hosts of protectors and warriors,
Show your kindness. Hear me now: be with me.
Bless me with your wishes.

Today I will take the Tirthika fortress.
I act only as your son.
I call on you, O warrior fathers.
KI KI KI LA. BU SWA. KI KI KI LA.

I call on the peaceful white lord of heaven's domain.
KI LI LI
Your helmet and armor are made of white crystal.
You ride a horse the color of moonlight.
On your right is a crystal arrow, on your left a crystal bow.
On your right a long-life arrow, on your left a spear;
On your right arm a tiger's mane, on your left a spotted leopard's
    skin.
Your horse's tail swirls like a blizzard,

And your brilliant white light pervades everywhere.
CHAO CHAO CHAO
Cut the Tirthikas' connection to the heavenly realm.
Let the winds of space descend and crush them to the ground.

I call on the fearless golden lord of the earth's domain.
SO LI LI SO
You sit on a golden throne wearing a helmet and armor of gold.
Your arrow on the right and bow on the left are golden.
On your right is a long-life arrow, on your left a spear;
On your right arm, a tiger's mane, on your left a spotted leopard's
    skin.
Smoke billows from the nostrils of your golden steed before you.
CHAO CHAO CHAO
Let the evil ones have no place on earth.
Raise mountains up beneath them and press them to the sky.

I call on the inscrutable turquoise lord of the domains below earth
    and sea.
CHA LI LI
You sit on a turquoise throne wearing turquoise helmet and armor.
Your arrow, bow, long-life arrow and spear are turquoise.
On your right and left arms you wear a tiger's mane and a leopard's
    skin.
Your horse, blue as the rolling ocean, prances before you.
CHAO CHAO CHAO
Fan the flames from beneath earth and sea.
Burn the earth-corrupters so no ash remains.

  The Tirthikas in the fortress perceive this song not as melody
and words, but as an unbearably sharp pain, as if sword points

pierce their ear drums and press into the center of their brains. Then, in turn, each of the warrior emanations begins to sing. First at the eastern gate, the Tiger warrior sings:

At the eastern tower of the flaming tongues of hatred,
O wisdom, kindle the fire,
Still the pain of birth.

And as he sings, the eastern wall bursts into flame. As they are being scorched and burned, the Tirthikas are pressed downward by a wind from the sky and upward by the earth itself and blood runs from their ears and nostrils. Many are destroyed on the spot, but some manage to drag themselves to the northern side.

At the northern gate, the Lion warrior sings:

At the northern tower of the black wind of envy,
O wisdom, kindle the fire,
Still the pain of old age.

The northern wall becomes a tower of fire. Those who can, run on; but many, many more die screaming, as they are caught and crushed by a great fist of wind, earth and fire joined together.

At the western gate, the Garuda warrior sings:

At the western tower of billowing lust,
O wisdom, kindle the fire,
Still the pains of illness.

And, as the western wall becomes a wall of fire, the ferocity of this tornado of horror becomes completely unbearable. Some are killed simply by the great roaring sound of the wind, which causes their brains to burst. Those who still somehow manage to survive crawl madly over rocks slippery with steaming blood to the one remaining bastion.

At the southern gate, the Dragon warrior sings:

At the southern tower of the immense cavern of pride,
O wisdom, kindle the fire,
Still the pain of death.

The southern wall collapses instantly in flames, and the former fortress has no existence other than as flame. Lungjag Nagpo and the few Tirthikas still alive are completely deranged. The root of their reality is cut completely, and their world is reduced to nothing but hideous suffering and torment. Their screams are delirious and inarticulate. Their blood vaporizes instantly and their bodies explode in the terrifying heat.

While the flames are still rising, and the Tirthikas still scream and scramble through the wreckage of their fortress, Gesar calls for a swarm of eagles, who remove the medicine treasury and place it on the roof of his palace in Ling. Also, as the citadel is about to collapse, Kyang Go Karkar resumes his original form and carries Padma Chotso to Shining Crystal Cave, where Gesar waits for her. They spend the next three days meditating, and when, at the end of that time, Gesar leaves, she remains.

Thus, the wind of their own anger, the earth of their own arrogance, and the fire of their own lust, when set free, destroy the bodies of Lungjag Nagpo and all the Tirthikas utterly. But their awareness, guided by the warrior songs, recognizes its own liberation and dissolves without hindrance into space. The great elements become peaceful, and the four emanation warriors return to Gesar.

v

When the ashes have cooled, Gesar returns to the Tirthika fortress. So fierce were the flames that nothing remains of the walls or the occupants, except an iron stronghold the size of a large room, which contains the treasury of the Buddha's teaching. Gesar shoots an arrow of meteoric iron at the structure and it shatters into a hundred pieces and the great collection of the Buddha's words is opened. Gesar takes the texts with him, and, in the guise of a pandit, he rides across Tibet and Nepal teaching from them.

6

Six months later, Gesar returns to Ling. Sechan Dugmo, his mother, the nobles, warriors and people of Ling are overjoyed with relief at his return, and a great banquet of celebration is held. The feasting goes on day and night, and Gesar, at last, recounts his conquest. But Todong, who is more than the worse for wear grumbles furtively, and, as time goes by, quite loudly. "Pooh. If everything you say is true, and if you have not just been traipsing all around while we, the elders of the tribe, myself foremost amongst them, have really been looking after the welfare of this kingdom, if you really have been accomplishing all these fine and important deeds, well, where, may I ask you, is the proof? Not just a lot of words, but some real proof. Something to show for all this supposed effort." Gesar sees that Todong is voicing something that others also have in their hearts. He takes them to the palace roof, and they see the bales upon bales of the thousand kinds of precious medicine. He shows them the texts which he has placed in his shrine room, and all are embarrassed at whatever doubtful thought they have harbored. But Todong finds himself the victim of yet another humiliation, and while feigning joy, his hatred of Gesar increases.

When the celebrations have ended, Gesar retires to his rooms to continue his meditation. His fate and that of the human realm are inseparable.

PART III

1

For many months, Gesar remains meditating in the solitude of his shrine room. Late one autumn night, when a wild cold wind roars through the sky, hiding the stars and making the crescent moon appear as a tiny boat tossed on a tempestuous sea, he looks out on the stone houses of Ling. Though here and there a faint wisp of smoke rising from the embers of a dying fire can be seen, the tribesmen of Ling are invisible, huddled in the shadows of their dark houses. The great range of mountains to the north is more a looming presence than something that can be clearly discerned, and the Lion Lord is pierced by a feeling of vast sadness at the fleeting nature of this life. Out of his longing and kindness, he sings this spontaneous song to the Great Rock Demoness, the legendary mother of his people, who presides over the Mother lineage of Dralas:

> From the unmoving and undivided brilliance of simplicity itself,
> At the zero point of life and death,
> You are the clarity of fury, the vibrance of passion,
> The wisdom of alternation.
> You are the essence of movement and blackness of ink.

You stand, as if running, on the back of a raven.
With the uppermost of your four gleaming snake-like arms,
You crush the sun and moon.
With your lower right hand, you eat the heart of duality
In which you take form.
With your lower left hand, you drink from a skull cup
Filled with a boiling ocean of poisonous thoughts.

You fly through the darkness of an empty sky
And your enormous wet mouth is open wide,
Displaying your four glittering iron teeth.
Your turquoise hair streams upward like a world-ending wind,
And your eyebrows and lashes blaze like the fire at the end of time.
From your three eyes, bloodshot and bulging,
Flash jagged swords of purple lightning.
You are completely naked: your breasts hang down,
And your dark genitals are exposed and open.

Alone since beginningless time, you are the cold wind
Shearing high peaks with razors of frozen air,
And shrouding mountain corpses in sheets of silver ice.
With your thunderbolts, you carve highlands and valleys
Into the face of the impassive earth.
When you shout with longing, avalanches dam the racing
    streams,
And lakes and green valleys spring to life.
Life here begins with your violent cry.
From the howling of your thunderous scream
Are born a million secret terrors.
Where there is struggle to survive,
You are the sharp essence of fear.

Nothing can hide from you,
And even the faint echo of your breath
Causes strokes, plagues, heart attacks and death.
You bring all to an end.

No rest, no stillness, no peace exists
That is not poised upon your gnashing fangs;
Nor warmth, nor growth, nor pleasant day
That is not clenched between your desolate angry claws.
The illusion of permanence is sustained by your breath alone.

With the slightest gesture of your long black arm,
The sky is cleared or filled with dark clouds,
The sun and moon shine or disappear.
As you dance alone and swirl in the empty air,
Vast, peaceful oceans become graveyards,
And lightning fires devastate the earth.
When your obsidian toe nails brush across the ground,
Ancient forests are shattered and their denizens crushed.
All that live on the earth or in the sea or air
Are forever at the mercy of your wild dance.

The beings who found themselves here in the Land of Snows
Cowered in terror of you, until one called on you
With gentle confidence and love. And from that love
You gave birth to a splendid race of brave men and women.
Just so, in the darkness of this time,
I call on you with longing untouched by frozen fear,
And offer love untouched by the hell-fire of hope.
In the realm where existence and non-existence do not part,
I offer up the subtle perfume of places and names.

In the realm where all motion is illusion,
I offer up the golden sky-flower of attraction and aversion.

In the realm where subject and object are not discriminated,
I offer up the bright torch of perception.

In the realm where chaos and order are one dance,
I offer up the delicious *torma* of conceptualization.

In the realm where ignorance and wisdom are inseparable,
I offer up the intoxicating liquor of individual consciousness.

With these offerings,
May we all enter the great dance of your wild embrace.
By the perfection of these illusory offerings,
Please be appeased and do not cast us off.

Since you are both existence and non-existence,
Let us not stray from wakefulness into the grip of the demon enemy.

Since you are both creation and destruction,
Let us not stray from wakefulness into the paths of hope and fear.
Since we cannot escape from you,
Let us be consumed in the bliss of your furious embrace.
Since the shadows of life and death have no meaning for you,
Please protect us with the light of unconditional confidence.

Since you cannot ever be appeased,
May confidence always expand like a silver sword
Cutting through the midnight sky.

Since you are the essence of genuineness,
May the life, mind and vow of Gesar, King of Ling

Reach its full measure in the great seal of confidence.

Since you are the essence of power,
May the life, mind and vow of the Rigden Kings
Confirm the strength and prosperity of this realm
And bring the Kingdom of Shambhala to this world.

Quickly, suddenly, O like the wind,
Great Furious Black One, come now, come.
Swiftly, swiftly make this be so.

And so, in the years that follow, born from mild breezes and warm spring rains, lush grasses swell in the valleys and many foals and calves fill the pastures of Ling. In summer, the noon sun shimmers on the ripening sheaves of grain, as on a golden ocean. In fall, the harvests are plentiful and herds of horses and cattle brought down from the high mountain meadows cover the plains. In the long, cold nights of winter, the people of Ling sleep secure in their warm beds, untroubled by want or fear. Their life together is harmonious and their disputes few.

In midwinter, late on a glittering frozen starlit night, when the new crescent moon has just returned to the sky, and Gesar sleeps dreamlessly in his palace bedroom, the goddess Manene comes to him. She descends across a bridge of faint moonlight, arching down from the lower point of the crescent moon directly into his heart. There she takes her place and sings to him:

i

Royal brother, Gesar, Great Warrior King of Ling,
Above you, the King of the Lha domain, youthful and vibrant

In crystal armor, rides on his snow-white horse,
While his lustrous pennants and those of his host of Drala warriors
Snap in the wind making the sound of cracking glacier ice,
He rides above you through the sky as your guide.

The Naga King of the Lu domain, powerful and wise
In turquoise armor, with his sea blue horse.
Sits beneath you in the deep caverns of his jewel palace.
His warriors and subtle emissaries
Moving ceaselessly and silent beneath sea and earth,
Confirm you with wisdom and wealth.

You, Gesar, in your golden armor
And starry chain-mail, with lightning sword, arrows of wind,
And your splendid horse of miracles, Kyang Go Karkar,
You sit in the place of the Lord of the Nyen domain,
Surrounded by your queen, your ministers,
Your generals and your hosts of brave warriors.
You radiate the protection of confidence throughout this land.

Your mind is ever vast and clear as the sky,
Your wisdom is ever bright and unwavering like the sun,
And your compassion ever clear and all-pervading as the moon.

ii

But, even the bravest warrior with the sharpest eye
Who finds himself in a dense forest on a moonless night
Is unable to see and may soon be lost.
Branches and thorns strike and cut him as he moves.

He may be attacked by serpents, wolves or worse:
He may find his mind prey to forgotten childhood fears.
He may be assailed by phantom terrors of all kinds.
He may feel he is going mad and he may lose his mind.
He may fall from a cliff he cannot see and lose his life.

This world, so rich in the bright promises of happiness,
Is in truth, O Lion King, just such a forest.
Here the sky is often filled with clouds.
By night it becomes black, and even the sun and moon
Are always moving and often disappear.
Love becomes brutal selfishness, wisdom becomes calculation,
Prosperity becomes rabid greed, and justice, a means of
    oppression.
No attainment is ever permanent here.
Even this kingdom, Sire, whose dignity and wealth you have
    restored,
Will fall and rise again a hundred times.
Even your own eternal wisdom, confidence and power
Will here be seen to wax and wane.
There will never be a time when genuine dignity is stable.
There is no place in which great exertion is not required.

iii

Even now, within Ling itself, Todong, among others,
Is filled with lustful thoughts and envious greed.
For him, this kingdom is merely a sensual playground
Which fills him with longing and desire.

His selfish grasping makes him an easy pawn of the demon lords,
So he smiles in his sleep only when he dreams of your death.

On the borders of Ling, in each of the four directions,
The four great demon lords send their emanations to undermine
    Ling.

From Lutzen, the twelve-headed demon of the North,
Come black winds of anxious doubt and jealous arrogance,
So that men's acts become based on efficiency and power.
When you destroy him, O Gesar,
You will suffer the loss of your mind,
But the orange banner of the Lion will fly victorious.
From the East, domain of the great demon tribe of Hor,
Come sly glittering blue waves of possessive deceptions,
Which lead men to act out of their impoverished ego fixation.
Before they are conquered, dear brother,
You will suffer the loss of your kingdom,
But the white banner of the Tiger will fly victorious.
From the West, the demon kingdom of Satham of Jang,
Come dazzling red clouds of hope and fear,
Enticing men to act out the entertaining dramas of self-involved
    passion.
In conquering them, kind friend, you will suffer the loss of your
    body,
And your great strength will not be of use,
But the red banner of the Garuda will fly victorious.

From the South, the realm of the demon Shingti,
Come sticky yellow dust clouds of uncertainty and theorizing,
Leading men to act with magnetic sophistry to overcome their

loneliness.
Before you can conquer them, stainless hero,
You must break your sacred oath,
But the blue banner of the Dragon will fly victorious.

iv

These demons and hordes of others like them
Are the ancient weaknesses of race and realm,
And, for all their innumerable forms,
They are the many-twisted branches of a single root.
They are the perverted face of liberation.
They are the belief that freedom can be possessed
As an experience, as power, intelligence, lust or wealth.
They are the rapacious struggle of the deluded mind
To expand the domain of its own projections.
Thus they undermine the true merit of men and nations,
Which is confidence in the power of egoless action.
The blazing sun of unbiased wakefulness
Becomes the shifting half-light of craving.

These demons enter through the gate of selfishness:
Careless followers become their unwitting slaves.
With a relentless appetite for confirmation and permanence,
They grip the minds and suck the marrow
Of those who madly seek fulfillment in their service.
They consume and waste the earth and all who dwell here.
Doubts, depression, pride and oracles are their feeding ground.
A poisonous, arid, hysterical claustrophobia is their residue.

To defeat them, you have entered their terrible realm
And must, Great Warrior King, endure their madness.

Demons cannot be attacked directly or conquered from afar.
As you entered their terrain when you accepted human birth,
They will enter you; they will erupt and slide into your thoughts
With their array of fears, arguments, enticements and promises.
Do not accept their conditions and do not ally yourself with
    them;
Remember your true allegiance, the unconditional confidence
Of the vast, clear midday sky.

v

To defeat the demonic lords,
You must stir up their innate paranoia
To separate them from the phenomena that support them.
You must stir up their innate lust
To separate them from those that love, counsel and follow them.
False hopes and fears must paralyze their acquisitive minds.
In this way, they lose their hold on the past, present and future.
Uprooted from time itself, they are destroyed.
In the very act of destruction, the armor of life is fulfilled.

Your life here, Great Fearless Friend of Man,
Is without comfort or ease. It is ceaseless warfare.
Again and again, you must rouse yourself and raise yourself up.
Again and again, you must rely only on your discipline.

Again and again, you must confirm your dignity.
You must raise the Tiger, Lion, Garuda, Dragon victory banner.
Conquest over demonic degradation must be re-enacted again
    and again.
You must uphold the sign of unfailing inspiration,
The all-victorious flag of the Great Eastern Sun.
This is the only path in this roiling sea of confusion
Called the human realm.
This is the only example, the only attainment,
The only joy and the only true glory.
This is the true warriorship that does not rely on results.
This is the continuous truth of your eternal kingdom.

Because, Lion King of Ling, you act in this way,
You are an unfailing, all-consuming torch,
Always alight in the hearts of men and women.
Even amid the black torments of fear, doubt, madness and despair,
The very mention of your name will restore human dignity forever.

These words of Manene's melodious song are heard only by
Gesar and tears fill his eyes as she glides up the moonlight
bridge, leaving a hollow sadness in his heart.

The next morning, at first light, Gesar dresses himself in full
armor and calls for his horse to be outfitted for a long expedition. He summons the people of Ling, and tells them, that now,
if Ling is to be secure, he must go to destroy Lutzen, the twelve-
headed demon of the North.

Because they remember how long he was absent before, his
wife, ministers, generals and warrior companions beg him to
return soon. In particular, his wife, Sechan Dugmo has a premo-
nition of disaster for the people of Ling, and begs him to make

his journey a short one since she fears that a long absence will bring the downfall of the kingdom. Gesar assures them all, as best he can, and he mounts his horse and vaults into the sky. He does not glance backward, but there is an ache of sadness in his heart.

2

Lutzen's deadly kingdom spreads across a vast high plain. In its center, there is a towering black mountain jutting abruptly out of the earth. On its peak, circled by three stone walls, is Lutzen's iron palace, wreathed in a solid mass of swirling gray clouds. Trails of sulphurous vapor pour down from these clouds, filling the land with freezing fog and hot trails of poisonous smoke.

The Lion Hero's breastplate glows like the sun and his helmet gleams like the moon, and his chain mail and weapons jingle like a joyful chorus of bells as Kyang Go Karkar canters across the plain. His mind is joyful as he enters into this conflict, and his discipline is crisp and sharp. He and his wonder horse leap as playfully through the shadowy rolling landscape as a snow lion bounding from peak to peak. But as they ride further into the demon's lethal realm, Gesar's armor seems to dull in the mist, and the sounds of horse and rider become muffled. As he rides through the fog, fleeting shadows of wolves or wild dogs race silently by, and the screams of vultures or animals being disemboweled pierce the dense gloom. Sometimes it seems as if large herds of cattle and long caravans of men are passing them invisibly nearby. As they ride on, huge, impressive stone structures like waiting empty fortresses loom up, and huge rusting iron engines of no known purpose materialize beside them as if from nowhere. The air is heavy with menace, intimidation and power. The hero's mind is increasingly filled with thoughts of longing for his homeland, for Sechan Dugmo, and for the good company of the people of Ling.

Suddenly an enormous soot-black bull with bloodshot yellow eyes and steaming breath rears up out of the shrouded earth before them. It halts, paws the ground, and, bellowing, charges. Gesar feels his face singed by the bull's burning breath, and the wonder horse wheels to avoid its steel horns. As they turn and face each other once again, Gesar sends three lightning-like arrows at the bull's heart, but to his shock, with a sound like wood striking stone, they merely bounce off the beast's hide. He is barely able to conceal his paralyzed discouragement as all his skills seem to desert him. The bull repeats his thundering attacks, and horse and rider wheel again and again, evading him.

"Are you so easily done in? What are you waiting for? Do you fall apart so easily? Are you only brave when you win easily? Are you helpless unless you are surrounded by adoring multitudes? Are you only confident when there is someone to see it? Shoot your longest arrow between its eyes," Kyang Go Karkar shouts breathlessly. And Gesar, as if waking from a stupor, speeds an arrow deep into the demon bull's brow. The body crashes as it falls and when Gesar rides on, its corpse evaporates in the steam.

By nightfall, Gesar is tired, and while he rests, Kyang Go Karkar leaps over the miasma to see what they must contend with next. On his return, he tells Gesar that they are near the base of the mountain, and encircling it are three rock rings. Guarding the first ring is an army of warriors descended from gods; at the next ring is an army descended from humans; and at the final one, an army of demons. Gesar smiles, eager to engage the enemy, and he mounts the miraculous steed, resolved to reach Lutzen's lair by nightfall.

As they ride through the low forests that cover the base of the mountain, their ears are assailed by terrible screams, moans and hissing curses, but when they reach the first ring of rock walls, called Pearl Ridge, the Lion Hero calls out:

"You who are sons of gods, why do you defend the vile thing within these walls?"

"If our master finds you here, you red-footed mortal, he will first flay and eat you and then he will kill us, so please, leave this place at once."

"I cannot, for I am Gesar, King of Ling, and I must kill your lord. The fear of death has never left even a fingerprint on my being, and I will destroy such fear in my domain."

"It is true that we have heard this prophecy."

"What has Lutzen done for you to make you stand in my way?"

"As children, against our parents' wishes, we went one afternoon to play in the fields of the human realm. Lutzen captured us, as he did the human guards on Golden Ridge, above, and because he keeps us alive we serve him. You may think us cowardly and petty, but you do not know Lutzen's power. When even the thought of him enters our mind, it makes us hopeless and afraid, for even when he looks at us, we feel as if we are being burned. It is unpleasant to say his name, for it makes us as uneasy as the thought of a painful death. As far as we are concerned, we do as he asks so that he will not think of us at all, and will continue to provide our sustenance."

"So if I free you and allow you to return to your own realm, will you help me?"

"We shall do as you say."

Gesar passes through their ranks and rides to the wall of Golden Ridge. There he speaks to the human guards as he had to the gods, and they all agree to let him pass and to help him. He forms the two troops into two lines, and knowing that any appeal to the demons of the topmost ring, the Black Ridge, is futile, he rises up on his great horse, high into the sky, and assaults the demon guards with thunderbolts and hailstones the size of boulders. Those demons who are not killed outright jump down from Black Ridge and are slaughtered by the troops of guards waiting below. Gesar sends the god and human soldiers on their way, and transforms himself and Kyang Go Karkar into a rock, so that they can examine Lutzen before they must fight him.

Soon enough, the black demon strides through the gates of his castle. He is as tall as three tall men and he has twelve heads, each with long brass fangs and each with glaring eyes of a different color. The heads bob and stare and snap in all directions on the end of his twelve long necks which are covered, as is his muscular body, with black metallic scales. With long powerful arms and silver-taloned hands, he resembles the Lord of Death himself. The demon roars in fury, bending trees to the ground, when he sees that his guards have bolted, and madly he races off to find them.

Gesar on his horse then strides nonchalantly into the court-yard of Lutzen's castle. There they are surprised to find that the demon's wife is an elegant and beautiful Chinese lady, who is staring down at them from her balcony. And she is no less surprised to see a handsome warrior in gleaming armor and fluttering pennants, seated on a restless powerful steed, suddenly in the middle of her domain.

"Stranger, no matter how brave, strong or handsome you may be, nor how skillful and strong your horse, it would be best if you left here at once. For this is the castle of Lutzen, the twelve-headed demon lord, whose power is total and anger continuous. His rule is as absolute as death and as all-pervasive as the fear of death. His way of life is simple: he terrorizes, paralyzes and kills. That is all.

"Today he is more furious than usual, and despite your obvious strengths, he will make a meal of you faster than his twenty-four eyes can blink." But Gesar merely smiles at her and makes no move, so she continues somewhat petulantly: "Well, if you insist on being a guest, I can assure you that you will end up as dinner. But you might as well tell me who you are, and why you have come here."

"O Queen, more beautiful than the smile of the moon, I am Gesar, King of Ling. My strength is eternal, and my warriors numberless. My lands take a hundred-days' ride to cross and my wealth cannot be counted by a dozen misers in a dozen days. I have come here to destroy your husband and put an end to his poisonous cruel realm. Will you help me?"

"I have heard Lutzen speak of you. You are the only being that introduces some hesitation into his mind, and I must admit that interests me, since he fears nothing at all. But as to helping you, why should I? It is true that Lutzen is vicious and harsh, but he has treated me well. He has devoured my rivals and always treated me with as much kindness as he is capable of. Besides, he may well defeat you, and then where would I be?"

"O Queen, you are as wise as you are delicious, but it has been foretold that I shall destroy your demon lord utterly. There is no doubt about that; but without your help, it will be most difficult. And I have much to offer you. When Lutzen is defeated, you will be free. You will have a great palace in my kingdom, with lands so extensive and retainers so numerous, that the very word "need" shall never arise. I will give you a hundred bolts of silk brocade and two trunks of precious stones.

"But more to the point, O precious Queen, how could I not love you? Your charm and beauty are wasted on this monstrous creature to whom an unjust fate has chained you. It does you credit that you have made the best of it, but I have seen your lord, and his embraces must at least be strange. Sometimes as he touches you, do you not think about a man's touch and a man's love? Do you not fear that the offspring of your union with your twelve-headed lord would resemble more a scorpion than anything you would care to see? Surely you dream of a child as beautiful as yourself."

Their conversation continues in this way, until after not too long a time, Lutzen's queen, who in truth has found the King of Ling attractive from first sight, agrees. She hides Kyang Go Karkar in the caverns beneath the castle, and leads Gesar by the hand into the demon's lair. There they spend the next few hours playfully. She hides Gesar under a copper pot in a hole beneath the floor, and tells him to listen carefully, for when Lutzen returns, she will trick him into telling how he may be destroyed.

Soon enough, the demon king returns, more sullen and enraged than ever since he has been able to find only one of his guards, a human whose corpse he has brought back with him to feed on. He is disturbed by the disappearance of his human and god-born guards, and upset by the slaughter of his demonic protectors. Could they have encountered someone more powerful and frightening than he? He is afflicted with a sense of ominous foreboding. He ignores his wife's greetings and fetches his oracle bones. The divination is bad. It is the name of Gesar of Ling, and for the first time in his long life, Lutzen feels a pin-prick of genuine fear in his heart. In a frenzy, he consults the oracle again and again before throwing the bones across the room.

"What is it, my Lord?"

"The guards have gone or disappeared. I cannot find them. And Gesar of Ling, the one who is to bring about my end, is near. The oracle says he is very, very near and in a small black hole deep under the earth."

"I have heard you speak of him before, but clearly, the oracle is showing you that he is dead and in his grave," is the frightened queen's quick-witted reply. The demon nods, thinking that she may be right, and he begins to feel his confidence returning. "But the oracle may mean that there is something else to fear. Your guards are gone, and I am very much afraid. There is no one to protect you now. My dear Lord, perhaps you should send to one of our powerful neighbors for help. Perhaps your own great strength is not enough." Then she clutches the demon and pretends to cry. Lutzen roars in fury.

"Fool, my body is protected in profound and subtle ways. Stop your awful wailing and do not doubt me. Before Gesar, if he is alive, or any other being can kill me, first he must kill my beautiful sister, seductive as the desire for death, the essence of my craving, who dwells at the summit of the Tree of Delight in the sky kingdom of the East. Then he must get possession of the emerald beetle, the seed of my life force, which is the belief in the reality of life and death. It is guarded by my hideous, cannibal-demon sister, terrifying as the fear of death, who is the essence of my wrath, in the sky kingdom of the West. Then he must come in the night and kill the golden fish of confidence that slips from my right nostril while I sleep and plays on my right shoulder, and the silver fish of consciousness that slips from my left nostril and plays on my left shoulder. And still I will not die until all my twelve heads are cut from my body. Judge for yourself, my gentle beauty, whether or not I am well defended. And for heaven's sake, stop your tears."

"There is nothing like you that walks upon the earth, nor soars through the sky, nor swims in the sea, and it is my great blessing to be your wife," she replies. So, pleased with her praises, the demon lies down to sleep.

The next morning, Lutzen leaves at first light, riding off on his copper-green mule in search of his guards. Not much later, Gesar rises into the sky upon the wonder steed. Within moments, they arrive at the Eastern sky kingdom. At the foot of the Tree of Delight, Gesar dismounts.

"How," he muses aloud as he stares at the silent and dazzling, emerald-like beauty sitting high in the tree, "how, can one so beautiful confine herself in a treetop? She is more beautiful than any human, and must be the daughter of a god or dragon lord, but cursed in some way that she must be imprisoned here."

"Well," thinks Lutzen's sister to herself, "Why should I? I'm not a bird, and there's no reason that I shouldn't go down and talk with this handsome young warrior." And so the demon beauty descends to the ground and stands smiling before the King of Ling. "What has brought you to this place, O Lord?"

"Your beauty, great lady, may be confined to this realm, but its fame exceeds the three worlds. I have come here to see and pay homage to you. I have brought you a golden necklace which once belonged to the great sea dragon kings." And he holds out a fine gold chain, but as she reaches for it he closes his hand. "No, O beautiful one. Please forgive my impertinence, but I have traveled far, and I will not be content unless I may adorn you with the necklace myself." The demon beauty smiles and bends her neck towards him. Quick as a flash of summer lightning, Gesar whips the chain around her neck and, holding an end in each hand, pulls it tight. She screams and thrashes as he strangles her, but at last falls dead to the ground. In that moment, her body loses the form of a beautiful woman and becomes that of a huge black serpent. Gesar sets fire to the corpse and the tree and sets off for the Western sky kingdom.

Lutzen, riding madly across the smoking plains of his domain feels a terrible pain in four of his heads as if they are filled with molten copper.

Gesar has no sooner arrived at the Western sky kingdom than

a yellow deer races across his path. He shoots the deer through the forehead, and his arrow lodges in the animal with the tip of meteoric iron protruding from its flank. Immediately, the deer is transformed into an immense cannibal-demoness, so huge that its upper lip touches the sky and its lower lip the earth.

"Who are you, bold warrior, that you have wounded me so?"shrieks the demoness.

"Why sister, do you not recognize me, your brother, Lutzen?" Gesar replies.

"Well, you have certainly changed since I saw you last."

"Since I have married a beautiful Chinese wife, I have changed my form to please her."

"So why did you wound me so with this cruel arrow, dear brother?"

"Out of hatred, dear sister, since you have guarded the beetle that is the seed of my life force from the day that I was born, and I have never even looked at it."

"I have only done so because I know your rash nature," whines the demoness, " and I don't wish any harm to come to you."

"If you show it to me now, I will pull out my arrow." The demoness sighs and hurls the wriggling green beetle at Gesar's feet, and he quickly crushes it with his foot. A noxious green-black inky fluid stains the ground. Then he seizes the feathered end of the arrow that protrudes from between the demoness's eyes, wrenches it around, plunges it down straight through her heart, and she falls to the ground dead. Gesar lights another great fire to consume the cannibal and the beetle, and returns to Lutzen's castle.

Lutzen returns soon after, screaming with anguish about the pain in eight of his heads, which feel as if they were being pierced by burning swords. He rolls on the floor, back and forth, until at last he falls asleep. After a while, just as he has said, two fish, one silver and one gold, emerge from his left and right nostrils and play on his shoulders. Gesar rushes out from his hiding place, and with a club in each hand, smashes them to pulp. Lutzen, feeling the mighty blows on his shoulders, wakes with a titanic roar. But Gesar, with his lightning sword swirling like the sun reflected in a whirlpool, decapitates eleven of the demon's heads before he can do a thing. From his remaining head, Lutzen implores Gesar to spare him, and swears that he will be his vassal. But Gesar sees that Lutzen's body is turning to bronze, and that the demon is simply waiting for his body to become invulnerable. He plunges his sword into Lutzen's chest, but when he withdraws it, it is covered with molten metal. Assaulting the demon with a whirlwind of blows, he manages to sever Lutzen's final head, and at last Lutzen is dead.

As she looks at his immense grotesque form lying still on the floor, Lutzen's wife feels a pang of remorse.

"Great Lion King, you have accomplished what no man ever could, and freed the earth from the infection of this demon. But this creature, for all his horrors, never did me any harm, and without my help, you could not have destroyed him with such ease. Would you then, as a favor to me, give my former lord the instructions that will enable him to be free in death?"

Gesar sees the request is just and in accord with his own purposes, and so he sits down beside the gigantic body and sings:

Lutzen, Demon Death Lord of the North,
I am Gesar, King of Ling.
Lutzen, Demon Lord of the North,
Because of me, you have known fear.
Because of me, you no longer rage in the limits of your form.
Because of me, now you enjoy the great natural freedom.

Lutzen, Demon King of the North,
I am Gesar, Lion King of Ling.

Together, we have played out a certain drama
Where you were a demon and I, a king.
Now, while I must continue to play out this part,
You are unfettered.

Fear and death are now self-liberated.
Your mind, dense with sensation, rage and guile,
Filled with death and embodying death,
Is now cut through,
Is now pure naked awareness.
Your dark and shifty realm of paranoia and rampant appetite,
Filled with fear and perpetuating fear,
Is now destroyed,
Is now limitless vast space.
While the seeming gap between space and awareness
Made you struggle for existence,
Now there is only the brilliance of limitless expanse.
Lutzen, do not toy with doubt or regret.
Rely on this alone.
The seeming opposition between life and death is now cut
    through.

You are now experiencing the true nature of all,
The hidden real aim and end of all actions,
The inner true quality of all desires.
Do not be tempted to resume your armaments.
Do not thrash or lunge or flee.
Simply rest in wakefulness.
Do not stir, for there is nothing to be achieved.
Simply rest in space.
There is no longer a container or anything to be contained.

This is the limitless brilliance of primordial wakefulness,
The heart essence of deathless life.

However vivid are the mirages arising in this great mirror,
Know that this mirror is mind.
Do not grasp at these phantoms of existence,
Recognize that this mirror is both mind and beyond mind.
Shine in this radiant mirror of confidence.
Rest in this sonorous mirror of eternity.
All is resolved in dazzling measureless freedom.
Open your heart, Lutzen, be confident.
Do not hold back. You are dissolved.

Where the atmosphere of the castle and the demon's kingdom had been threatening, dank and full of mists, suddenly it is clear and clean. The demon's wife cries out:

"O Lion King of Ling, more sustaining than Mount Sumeru, you have destroyed the demon and all his minions, and brought true liberation into the heart of what was once a dark land. Please drink this cooling wine, for you are entitled now to rest and ease for all your weariness." Gesar's desire for relief is indeed at that moment very great and she gives him a dark drink in a golden cup. But the wine is filled with the opiates of many impure substances, which cloud Gesar's mind. His kingdom, his purposes, even his own personality become like a vague and distant dream.

The queen now keeps him as her husband, and together they play at being king and queen of their northern kingdom. Forgotten by Gesar, Kyang Go Karkar is kept hidden in the dark caverns far beneath the castle, where he is fed on meager rations of rotten grass. The miracle steed becomes a dusty shadow, barely able to stand, as Gesar lives for six long years in dreamy mental stupor.

3

But in the darkness of the night, Kyang Go Karkar, though his once lustrous body is feeble, remains in heart clear and strong. Though he dwells in the depth of sadness, he still smells the distant joyful breeze. And each night in the dark, he sings this song:

Though faint and from far off,
I smell the fragrant seasons turn in the night:
Bright on the air, the new thistle crown,
The new-mown hay, smoke and drying leaves,
The first crystal of ice on a black lake.
Bats, barnswallows, burrowing mice, gray cats and buzzing flies
Wander, stalk, hide, fly and gossip.
Like shining drops of dew suspended in the air,
Worlds of light held together on an invisible web,
All this is the dazzling multiform display,
The magic of coincidence.
But neglected and uncelebrated,
This is a fallow field choked with weeds and idle thoughts.

My neighs and whinnies of longing and sadness
Do not wake the Lion Lord, who has forgotten me;
Stir no true joy in the one who sleeps
Deep in the embrace of the dreams of need.

The promises of spring, the luxury of summer,
Satisfaction of autumn and deep stillness of winter
Follow the sun's progress through the sky,
Are pulled by the ebb and flow of the moon,

Are touched by a mysterious array of demons, beasts, and gods
In the constellations of the night.
So the quickness of life expands
In the luscious scent of ripening love,
Stirring fury, the feeling of an unanswered question,
The fear of an uncertain end.
These subtle and profound rhythms
Are the calls of uncontrived affinity,
And fill our hearts with endless longing.
These are the resonating power of magic.
But if there is no deep passion and no self-discipline,
This great music flies across the earth like a wanderer
Wasting his life talking to himself.

My neighs and whinnies of longing and sadness
Do not wake the Lion Lord, who has forgotten me;
Stir no true joy in the one who sleeps
Deep in the embrace of the dreams of need.

A vibrant, blazing rainbow palace, spanning a grassy plain,
Is undivided from those who chance to see it;
A lone dog barking in the night is inseparable from the night
And from a distant hearer.
A stillness before sunrise, before the open-eyed birds take flight,
Stops a solitary wanderer.
A horse and rider flying on muffled hooves
Through silent swirls of sparkling wet snow
Are indivisible in a single moment.
So, in the motionless center of all the vivid events of duality,
There is the cold tart taste of the well spring of nonduality,
The deep and mysterious abiding origin of magic and life.

But when there is reliance on racing thoughts and sedative obsessions,
Then the vivid mind of nonthought becomes a sky without
   rainclouds
And the world of men is without peace,
A wasted, barren storm of dust.

My neighs and whinnies of longing and sadness
Do not wake the Lion Lord, who has forgotten me;
Stir no true joy in the one who sleeps
Deep in the embrace of the dreams of need.

And here imprisoned in this dark, musty cave
Is Kyang Go Karkar, the great windhorse,
Born spontaneously out of the net of the world's phenomena,
The ever-present energy of nowness,
The self-arising wisdom of coincidence.
My body is doubtlessness, my legs are miracles,
My mane is gallantry, my silky tail delight.
My heart is a mountain stream of longing.
When I am unridden,
The power of genuineness dissipates.
When I am riderless,
All the virtues of the human realm degenerate.
The traditions of true human dignity are abandoned.
Brothers quarrel, wives stray, children are neglected,
Elders are left to rot.
Rulers act only for personal gain,
And power is sought only for its own sake.
Everything and everyone becomes an object of exploitation,
People no longer respect their own inheritance.
Their world is a lurid hallucination of hollow time.

My neighs and whinnies of longing and sadness
Do not wake the Lion Lord, who has forgotten me;
Stir no true joy in the one who sleeps
Deep in the embrace of the dreams of need.

But even as Gesar is content, living like an automaton, enjoying his new wife and daily riding out on Lutzen's copper-green mule to hunt, the sound of Kyang Go Karkar's song burrows deep into his heart while he sleeps, and as the years go by he becomes slowly more anxious and ill at ease.

4

One morning as he stands on the balcony of the palace, staring disconsolately at the sky, a large brown falcon alights on the balustrade not far from him. At first it appears that the falcon has tucked its head beneath its wing, but as Gesar looks, he sees that the falcon has no head, and he is all the more startled when the falcon first sings a song and then speaks to him:

When the Lion Lord had vanished from his throne,
Doubt and depression became the true lords of Ling.
When the queen of Ling thought no more of her throne,
Self-cherishing and empty ritual became a way of life.
When the ministers thought only of their own survival,
When the warriors were dispersed,
Confidence in the warrior path became mere longing,
And a sloppy recital of distant days was all that remained to
     celebrate.
In secret, we of Ling do not care if we are alive or dead.

"Gesar, Lion Lord and King of Ling, you who have abandoned all that you strove for, all those who loved you, and all those who relied on you, are you so lost that you do not recognize me?" Gesar, who cannot tell if he is dreaming, shakes his head. "I am Gyaza, son of Singlen, former King of Ling, whom you were pleased to call a brother and a friend." Gesar is suddenly shocked as his whole life in Ling floods suddenly back upon him. He is flustered and can barely speak.

"Gyaza, Gyaza, my brother, my friend, how have you come to take this terrible form? What has happened?"

"Six years have passed since you set out to destroy Lutzen, and none in Ling has heard a single word of you in all that time. It was not known that you had found another queen and kingdom; it was thought you were destroyed. And perhaps it would have been better if that were so, for Gesar, in your absence, Ling has been conquered by Kurkar, the white demon king of Hor, whose great silver shield is marked with a cockerel, and his brothers Kurser, the pale demon lord whose great brass shield is marked with a boar, and Kurnag, the black demon lord whose great iron shield is marked with a serpent. Your wife has been captured and now is married to Kurkar and is queen of Hor; most of your warriors and champions, I among them, have been slaughtered, and Todong, who reigns in your stead, keeps your mother as a serving maid. I am in this headless body since my own head was severed from my neck by Kurkar, demon king of Hor, and it now hangs over the gate of his palace as a warning and talisman. Until this severed head be buried in the ground, I cannot resume a normal form or human birth. I have taken birth in this form so that I might find you and bring you back to avenge the people of Ling."

On hearing this, Gesar cries out and in anguish strikes his head repeatedly on the stone parapet.

"How, oh, how can this be?"

"Having so recently returned to your senses, please stop in this effort to lose them again. Stop and listen to this bitter tale:

"Six years ago, Kurkar, demon king of Hor, decided he should find a wife. He sent a fox to the kingdoms of the human realms of the South, a hawk to the East, and a raven into Ling to the West to see if any members of the royal families there would be suitable. The hawk and the fox found many beautiful ladies, but all had one defect or another, and only the raven could tell of a perfect candidate, Sechan Dugmo, who was even then presumed to be your widow. The three demon brothers then transformed themselves into a single great vulture: Kurkar was the snowy head; Kurnag, its yellow body; and Kurser, the black wings and tail. They flew to Ling to see the lady, Sechan Dugmo. And when she saw the great vulture circling her tent, she knew it was an evil thing and begged the men of Ling to shoot it, but they would not. So the great vulture, having seen that Sechan Dugmo was perfect in every way, soared back to Hor, and the brothers assembled their hordes and invaded Ling to seize her.

"When Todong heard of the invasion and its purpose, he advised the warriors of Ling to surrender Gesar's wife and so avoid war. But they would not, and in the great battle that followed, the forces of Hor were thrown back. But then Todong, seeing an opportunity to become the ruler of Ling, went to the enemy camp and showed the Hor demons how to defeat Ling in exchange for the promise that he would be the viceroy. So the warriors of Hor, following Todong's advice, made it seem that they were retreating, and hid until the armies of Ling were dispersed. Then they returned and slaughtered all, including me, who tried vainly to resist. Todong was installed as lord of Ling, and Sechan Dugmo was taken to the Kingdom of Hor.

"For two years, Sechan Dugmo was able to put off Kurkar's insistent marriage plans. But with Todong advising Kurkar, her many strategies for delay were overcome, and at last she had no choice. She married Kurkar of Hor, who loved her and treated her with great kindness. Over time, she came to love him, and now she cannot bear the thought that you might be alive. Todong rules in your palace, and while he has amassed great wealth, the people of Ling grovel in poverty and can barely survive from season to season. The remaining warriors of Ling are dispersed and survive by farming. This, my brother and Lord, is the legacy of your sojourn here, all spent to content a demon's former wife."

Then Gesar's confusion is lifted, and he weeps a black torrent of bitter tears. At last he realizes how painful and hopeless it is to be mired in this treacherous world. Despite the impeccable power of his true nature and the purity of his intent, he has not escaped betraying himself and those he holds most dear. "How I have wronged you all: my brother, my peerless wife, my great warriors, my loyal friends!" And so loud is his cry that it reaches deep into the dungeon where Kyang Go Karkar is tied. Upon hearing that cry, the wonder steed breaks his bonds. He crashes through his prison's wooden gate, and with a mighty roar, berates his master.

"Now that your wits have been restored, can you do nothing better than howl to the heavens like a beaten slave? Put on your armor, lift up your sword, your bow, your lance. Put this lady here in a cave retreat for the rest of her days, that she may make amends for her selfish guile. Ride with me now to Ling so that we may plan the way to repair the remains of what your negligence has undone."

The headless falcon flies off into the sky as horse and rider speed home to Ling.

5

Even before they reach Ling's borders, the news of Gesar's return begins to spread. So by the time they reach Gesar's palace they are accompanied by a great host of warriors and citizens, and are met there by an even greater number of the same. Todong, hearing of Gesar's arrival and unable to escape, hides in an empty leather grain bag. Todong's family fawns on Gesar, even when he insists on using the bag in which Todong hides for a mattress. While he sleeps, Gesar kicks and punches his hiding uncle who, when he is dragged out into comparative freedom the next morning, is groggy, and black and blue. Todong stammers out justifications about thinking him dead and preserving Ling, but Gesar, outraged, stops him and has him locked in prison.

"Todong, perhaps your sly evasions will sound different, even to you, after a long time by yourself. I will not look at you, nor will anyone speak to you, until the conquest of Hor is done and Sechan Dugmo returned to this palace." Then Gesar turns to address all the warriors and people of Ling who have assembled in the night and waited for him at the palace. When he looks at them, he sees that their bodies have become skinny and their clothes ragged. On all their faces are the marks of hardship and want. Many who were familiar and dear to him are gone, and Gesar weeps as he sees this.

"Dear and loyal friends, you warriors and subjects who have lived in this kingdom, who have pledged your lives to me and have looked to me for protection in this world, the joy in your faces, as you look at me once more, fills me with sorrow and remorse. In a moment of fatigue, my mind was enslaved by a hungry demoness, and you have suffered terribly. In an instant of idle longing, my mind was paralyzed and this kingdom brought to degradation and ruin.

"Dear and loyal friends, that is the harsh way of this world. What you have lost is gone forever. What I have done cannot be undone, and so we must begin anew.

At the source of all appearance
Is the perfect mirror of nowness,
Utterly unstained by regrets of the past or fears for the future.
In the mirror's core, in the heart of all life,
Burns the fire of an eternal sun.
In the heartbeat of all beings
Cuts the self-existing sword of confidence.

Because you are true warriors,
Despair is your call to basic goodness;
Doubt is the razor knife of clarity.
From your unrequited love springs vast vision.
From your unappeasable longing has risen
The constancy and discipline that shall restore the world.

"Only your longing and faith have brought me back. Only your longing and faith have preserved the genuine goodness of our land. Only because you have kept your natural inheritance ever bright, even as a tiny ember in your heart, can we begin afresh. The Kingdom of Ling and the reality of enlightened society shall be all-victorious."

Gesar than tells the long tale of his conquest of the demon Lutzen, of his imprisonment, of his awakening, and of his return to Ling. The people of Ling exult as Gesar recounts his victory, and they weep as he tells of his subjugation. The thought of their

Lord's degraded circumstances join with their own bitter losses, and it seems that the rivers of their tears could fill a broad lake. When he has finished his story, dancers perform the dance called, "The Lion Bounds Over Life and Death."

Part IV

The next morning, Gesar announces to his people that in order to restore the glory of Ling, he will set out immediately to destroy the Kingdom of Hor. His people are overjoyed to hear of this, but many, recalling the terrible times which came in Gesar's last absence are afraid. For this reason, Gesar invokes the supreme protection of the Great Nyen, Magyel Pomra, by singing this song, called, "The Morning Sun of Nowness":

1

i

Running like rats in mazes we ourselves have made,
Terrified or lusting in the phantasmagoria of thoughts,
Bound in inextricable knots of love and hate, flailing,
Blaming the earth and polluting the elements with
  capricious rage,
Using spiritual practice for escape or self-justification,
With every rasping breath, we animate a landscape of total war,
Where living corpses gnaw at the flesh of the living and the dead.

In the rotting marketplace of fate, ghost-men and demon-women
Perpetuate their logic legacies of madness and barter their hearts

To grasp at broken mirrors, where yet they may find a face.
Desperately they traffic in promised joys, filling dog-carts of sorrow
For their lost children to drag across abandoned parks.

In this world, which is a burning iron cage,
Silent wails and shattering screams inflame the air,
As in the smoky dark, tongues lick at the molten bars.

But still, at the core, in the flickering half-light of this swirling hell,
Deep longing is the breath in these self-serving cries;
Clarity is the light shaped here as sorrow.

So in the empty chambers of our wounded hearts,
In the rhythm of our tormented breath,
In the yearning essence of our violent speech,
In the roiling storm-clouds of hallucination
That mask your indestructible domain,
We call to you, O Great Drala Protector,
We search for you, O Kindly Guide, O Lord of Nyen.

ii

Now, O Protector, in this cruel time of unspeakable degradation,
Come to us, arise in our hearts.

From your land of 360 towering snow peaks,
Ever brilliant and cool as the spontaneous thought of peace,
Please arise.

From your crystal stupa palace,
Whose tip pierces the invisible summit of the sky,
Whose base reaches the motionless core of existence,

And which is the radiance of life force itself,
Please arise.

From your throne of five-colored rainbow light,
Which is the spontaneous presence of wisdom display,
Great Magyel Pomra, Drala Lord of Nyen,
Mountain Lord of the East, Lord and Life of majestic Amnye
    Machen;
You who hold great Gesar's weapons that subjugate aggression,
The diamond vase of eternal life shines hidden in your heart.
Now rise up in the great mirror of nowness.

Swift protector, Magyel Pomra,
Rise up on your snow-cloud steed with its turquoise mane.
Rise up in a shower of sparks.
Through the swollen clouds of smoke and torment,
Be with us now.

Show yourself as the self-existing protector,
The unfailing wisdom guide in the essence of all delusions.
Rise up, and be with us now as essence and armor,
The strength of goodness, alive in body, speech and mind.

AH YA YA JHA

iii

Obliterating darkness and dimming all earthly fires,
Riding on the wind of the breath of life, suddenly you appear.
You burst into the eastern sky
Like the bright morning sun shining in a hurricane's eye.

Your powerful body is white as a conch and bears all the marks of
    a hero.
Your golden armor blazes and its crystal fittings sparkle.
Your jewelled cloak of white silk swirls around you.
Tied with a red silk scarf at your neck,
You wear the mirror which reflects all phenomena
And the vajra of indestructible wakefulness.
Your youthful face is peaceful and kind.
Your expression is lordly and uncompromising.
You wear a golden helmet, a moon sapphire in its center,
Surmounted by fluttering silver pennants.
In your right hand, you hold aloft the treasury of wisdom,
Bound in red and marked with a gold garuda.
In your left hand, you hold a crystal bowl of jewels
Heaped up around a crystal vase of deathless *amrita.*
On each of your fingers are rings of *gzhi.*
In the crook of your left arm is an iron lance
Bearing a rainbow banner swirling across the sky.

With your bow made from the foreleg of a black antelope
And arrows adorned with red garuda feathers,
You pierce the heart of fear, whether near or far off.
With your steel snare, you capture even secret passions,
And with your hooked knife, you cut off all thoughts at the root.
On your snow-white steed with billowing turquoise mane,
You fly across the sky as on a cloud before the wind.
No distance, whether in space or time, obstructs you.

You are accompanied by your young and radiant queen,
Who descends to the earth like the milky light of the full moon,

Riding a brown stag and bearing a mirror and a vase of *amrita*.

You are accompanied by your nine fearsome sons,
Riding horses, brandishing weapons,
Who fall on the earth like a hurricane laying waste to a forest.

You are accompanied by your nine enticing daughters, riding on birds
And carrying vases of purifying water and long-life arrows,
Who fill the sky with piercing omens and melodious songs.

Your three hundred and sixty fierce Ma brothers surround you.
They ride on tigers, leopards, jackals, horses
And on the backs of all untamable beasts.
They flicker through all the shadows of existence,
Brandishing arrows, iron lances, battle axes and bronze hammers.

The great queens of the four directions, majestic and nonchalant,
Dressed in crowns and silk brocades of blue, yellow, red and green,
Float above the cardinal points of your retinue.
They purify the four great elements
And seal the goodness of the whole expanse of space.

With the hissing sound of a flying arrow, with the shriek of a
    vulture,
With the roar of a tiger, with a crash of thunder, with a great shout,
You break through the smoking walls of deception and terror.

Indestructible display of nowness beyond thought,
With the power of goodness as your attributes and retinue,
You are with us now.

SAMAYA JA

iv

Great protector, Magyel Pomra,
You who protect life force in the human realm,
Please open your domain in every beating heart.
Great protector, Magyel Pomra,
You who rouse the splendor of confidence,
Please take your seat wherever there is yearning.

Encompassing all material and mental phenomena,
We make offerings, both imaginary and real.
Please accept them and take your seat here.

On a felt cloth, white as a serene mountain peak,
On an eight-petaled lotus of unshakable compassion,
We offer the white *torma*, made from all that sustains and enriches
The goodness of life in this world.

We offer the *amrita* of great bliss, beyond thoughts of life and death.
We offer the life blood of the world of life and death.
We offer *tormas* made from the countless kinds of karmic actions,
Which have solidified in the dramas of evil and good.

We offer the clear water that penetrates and purifies.
We offer the five senses and their objects of enjoyment.
We offer the seven treasures of a universal monarch,
And the eight auspicious symbols of unconditional enlightenment.

All this is surrounded by a splendid array
Of food, weapons, gold, jewels, and silk brocades.

Great Nyen, please accept all this
As the spontaneous enjoyment of your pure domain.

By accepting these offerings, O stainless kind Lord,
Please enter the whole of this world as your dwelling place.
Take the outer, inner and secret nature of our being as your seat.
Sealed by our prostrations and praise,
May our life be inseparable from the luster of your confidence.

O Great Nyen, Magyel Pomra,
Radiant, unwavering, self-born protector
Please remain here, ever inseparable from life force itself.

OM AH VAJRA-KULE MILMEN SAPARIVARA
IDAM BALIM TE KHA KHA KHAHI KHAHI

v

O Supreme Protector, Lord of Nyen,
You who are one with the aspirations of the Imperial Rigdens,
And bound with us in the samaya command of Gesar and
    Padmakara,
In this darkest time of torture and distrust,
Now is the time to act.
Now is the time to burn the masks of samsara's deceit from inside
    out.
Now is the time to proclaim the good realm of your
spontaneous display.

So that our hearts not sink in black clouds of sorrow and depression,
Protect every breath as the quickness of unconditional wakefulness.

So that fear and rage not bind our body with ropes of ice,
Resolve all outer obstacles into natural mindfulness.
Protect spontaneous courage in the white element of consciousness.

So that ruthless passions not run in our veins like molten copper,
Resolve all inner obstacles into natural awareness and
  compassion.
Protect spontaneous openness in the red element of
consciousness.

So that the poverty of ego fixation not blacken and foul the world,
Resolve all secret obstacles in the clear sun of centerless confidence,
That is primordially free from cause and effect,
That is not sustained by confirmation or result.
Protect the luminous mirror of nowness in the core of all.

O Magyel Pomra, Lord of Nyen, Protector of Life Force,
Accompanied by your numberless retinue of Drala and Werma
  friends,
Riding above landscapes made from outer, inner and secret offerings,
Encompassing mountains of *torma* made from flesh and blood,
Flying over lakes of pure water and oceans of intoxicating liquor,
Coursing on white clouds of pungent incense,
Now, in this very place,
Here, in this very instant,
Fill the pure sky of nowness
With the blazing light of the morning sun.

Blazing in the swirling veils of vicious torment,
Be the spontaneous white light of enduring peace.

Blazing in the thick veils of degraded poverty,
Be the spontaneous golden light of limitless enjoyment.

Blazing in the hot veils of desperate craving,
Be the spontaneous vermilion light of all-encompassing compassion.

Blazing in the enveloping veils of malicious envy,
Be the spontaneous rainbow light of all-victorious
   completion.

Riding on the eternal breath of life
Through the open sky of primordial awareness,
Great Protector, Magyel Pomra, with your dazzling retinue,
Burn the ground of the dark forest of universal karma.

And in the play of the Great Eastern Sun,
Let the boundless realm of purified phenomena
Ceaselessly sparkle, dance and shine,
Like a golden ocean of deathless wisdom bliss.

KI KI SO SO SAMAYA SO

At this song, joy and confidence blaze like a prairie fire in the
hearts of the people of Ling, and surrounded by his warriors,
Gesar rides out to conquer the Kingdom of Hor and the demon
lords of the East.

2

As they reach the borders of Hor, the landscape is covered with
banks of white snow, soft and lovely and tinted with pale shades
of pink, yellow and blue from the approaching dawn. Gesar
speaks to his men:

"The borders of Hor must be cleared of their protectors, so
that we may come and go without alerting the demonic lords of

this place, and so that when the time comes, you may return to destroy the demons themselves. I need your help now and will need it again after the defenses of this realm have been utterly undermined.

"In the interim, there is no one who can help me. The powers of the Hor demons are great and subtle. Kurkar, King of Hor, is more handsome than any man and only his bright red lips and silver teeth betray his demonic nature. His manner is appealing, quite grand, very magnetic, and instinctively, one wishes to please him. In this way, he takes possession of peoples' minds. His subjects come to live on the basis of their enthusiasm, and their only loyalty is to an uncertain future happiness, which they fervently pursue. They come to feel that to live in this way is a matter of simple logic. His brother Kurser is golden, shiny and obese. One feels a sense of complacency and contentment in his presence, and his influence causes the people of Hor to desire possessions and to fear their loss. Kurnag is small, fierce and violent. His black teeth are very long and his eyes are always bloodshot. He finds threats everywhere and takes pride in his energetic ability to forestall them. He confirms the fears of the subjects of Hor, even as they come to feel that his actions alone can protect them.

"Kurkar attracts, Kurser holds, and Kurnag protects, and all three together bind the legions of self-seeking beings whom they possess. To undo their work and render them vulnerable, I must enter their kingdom modestly. I must keep to the shadows like a tiger stalking its prey, and from time to time pounce when they are vulnerable. Humbly, quietly, patiently and slowly, with a coat of a thousand smiles, I must undo their confidence, so that at the proper time, they may be destroyed."

And so saying, Gesar and his men proceed into the sparkling display of the Land of Hor.

They travel for a day through this cloud-like scene when all at once a huge albino bull with red eyes, bloody mouth and fiery breath charges them. As Gesar and the warriors scatter, they unleash a shower of arrows at the beast, but none can penetrate his hide. Gesar directs the warriors as they divide into four groups. Each come at the bull from a different quarter, throw ropes around its legs, and pull it down into the snow until it suffocates.

Another day's ride into the shifty dazzling terrain, and they come to a black river on whose bank lives a large tribe of demon boatmen. This tribe ferries across those visitors who are welcome in the Kingdom of Hor. But if the visitors are uninvited or unwelcome, the boatmen drown them and steal their goods and horses. They are both the second line of defense for the kingdom and the source for all information about travelers in Hor. Gesar leaves his troops hidden on the riverbank and when he is out of their sight, he takes on the appearance of a traveling monk leading a large herd of phantom pack animals: horses, mules and yaks, all carrying bales of silks and goods for trade. He tells the chief of the boatmen that he is leading the way for a great lama and eight wealthy merchants, who will follow when he has crossed the river. Though slightly suspicious, the demon boatman cannot resist the prospect of robbing such a rich caravan, and so agrees to load Gesar's goods onto his boats. No sooner are the hundred boats, heavily laden, in midstream, than a storm suddenly descends upon them and overturns them all. The bedraggled demons swim to the shore, where the warriors of Ling descend on them and kill them all.

Then Gesar addresses the warriors of Ling:

"We do not have the strength to confront all these demons now. So for now, please return to Ling, strengthen yourselves, raise your children, and tend to your herds and fields so that we shall have, in three years time, the power to crush them. Meanwhile, I will undermine the demons' powers in the heart of their realm. Though you and I will be apart, and our activities different, we are moving as one being to one aim.

"When all is ready, I will call for you. Do not doubt it."

Gesar then proceeds alone to the silver palace of Kurkar of Hor. There he transforms himself into a servant, and creates a magnificent caravan encampment on the meadow before the palace. Kurkar is dining with his brothers when a slave comes to tell him of the caravan. Kurkar is surprised to hear of such a splendid array within his domain, particularly as he has not been warned by his border guards, and he sends out a soldier who tells the disguised Gesar that since the caravan has no permission to camp there, everyone must leave. Gesar replies to the impudent messenger that the caravan belongs to a great lama from India, and that they have come from far away to make offerings to the demon lord of the East. On hearing this, Kurkar sends out Sechan Dugmo to greet the travelers. Joy and sorrow mix in Gesar's heart, but do not sway him from his purpose, and, on behalf of his supposed masters, he sends boxes of gifts to her husband.

When Kurkar opens the packages, he finds a pair of earrings for his wife, a golden saddle and a golden bridle, two iron chains attached to a huge iron nail, eight copper nails and a sword of meteoric iron. "These are strange gifts," Kurkar says to his brother Kurnag, and the ever-wary brother replies:

"I think they have a hidden meaning. They are not tokens of friendship, but bearers of veiled threats. It may be that Gesar of Ling still lives and works his magic. If so, he means to put the saddle and bridle on you and drive you from Hor—they are portents of your subjugation. The chain will help enemies invade your castle; the nails driven into the hearts of your generals and ministers. The sword will bring down lightning-like assaults on this land, and the earrings mean that Gesar will recapture Sechan Dugmo."

"No, my brother, you are quite wrong. Just look at how beautiful and strange they are. Certainly we have never seen anything quite like them here," says Kurkar, who never doubts his appetites. "Tomorrow we will go see for ourselves who has sent these things and what they mean." But the next day, when they go to visit the caravan, it has disappeared entirely.

One week later, the daughter of a smith discovers a five-year-old boy playing in a garbage heap near the palace. She takes the child home to her father, and soon, because he is an exceptionally clever and able child, he is helping the smith at his work. And soon after that, he is forging things beyond even the elderly smith's ability. Gesar has transformed himself into this boy, and in this way he works his way quietly and secretly towards the destruction of the demons of the East.

The smith brings some of the child's work to Kurkar, and tells him about the remarkable boy. The king, intrigued, asks to see the child, but commands that first the child must make something surprising and wonderful for him. He provides a considerable quantity of gold, bronze, silver and copper for that purpose. While the child works these precious metals at the forge, he sings over and over:

Let the mind of grasping
Seize on little things as great.
Let the mind of fascination
Jump from one thing to the next.
Let the mind of attachment
Lose its grip on this earth.
Let the image of a true kingdom

Paralyze those who believe in a false one.
May the self-love of these demons
Be sated and stupefied by the shadow beings I devise.

In three days' time, the boy sends a message to Kurkar that he is done, and that after the work has been collected and if it is acceptable, he will present himself to the demon lord. It takes the servants a whole day of coming and going to carry the boy's creation into the palace; for with the gold, he has made a lama and a thousand smaller monks who listen to him as he lectures; with the bronze, he has produced a king surrounded by seven hundred courtiers to whom he is giving discourses on the law; with the silver, he has made a hundred dancing maidens who sing melodiously; and with the copper, he has fashioned a general and ten thousand soldiers whom he exhorts to bravery. Also, the boy has made out of conch, three thousand horses for all the leading personages.

When they have been set up before the king and his court, these magic dolls begin to move and act as real people. Kurkar, and his brothers, consorts, ministers, generals and officials are utterly fascinated by the doings of the miniature kingdom and watch them for hours, forgetting even to eat and drink. But while they are so carried away, Gesar resumes his true form and calls for Kyang Go Karkar.

Invisible to every eye, horse and rider leap into the sky and demolish the four ancestral patron gods of Hor: one they crush as they demolish the mountain peak where he lives; one they destroy by causing an avalanche to fall on his palace in the hills; one they destroy by diverting a stream; and the last they destroy in the sky with thunderbolts. All this is done in less time than it takes to tell it, and Gesar, in his guise as the smith's apprentice is scarcely missed. At the end of the evening, the dolls return to their original formation and sleep as real beings do.

In the night, Gesar sends a dream to Kurkar. The first among the ancestral gods rides before him on a towering thundercloud and requests that all the people of Hor have a sporting contest in his honor. "Do this and you will become as I am now," says the god. And in the morning, Kurkar and his two brothers make preparations to fulfill this seemingly auspicious prediction. Throughout the day, the warriors of Hor compete in horse races, archery contests and wrestling, and the best of them all, their greatest warrior, is an immense and powerful giant. He is victorious in all the contests, but as Kurkar is about to award him the victory prize, a small voice challenges. "Oh, he's not so great as all that. I'm sure I could do better." Everyone is shocked, and all the more so when a young boy swaggers out from behind a tent to challenge the giant. Kurkar knows that this must be the smith's apprentice and feels a foreboding chill, even as everyone else is laughing.

"If you are the smith's miraculous apprentice, I am indeed in your debt. But if you wish to fight against the greatest of our warriors, then I will not have you for long, and I would surely hate to lose you."

"O great King, I would not have said so myself; but indeed, if you mention it, you may have some small obligation to me. And if you wish to honor your debt, only let me fight this big oaf on the sole condition that if someone is killed, there will be no blood money owed." Kurkar, hoping that the giant will simply make a fool of the boy and let it go at that, nods his approval. The giant is humiliated to be fighting a mere boy and tries to end it quickly, but he finds himself tripped up and on the ground, time after time. Finally the huge warrior makes an enraged furious lunge at the boy, but Gesar trips him up again, and his head crashes down on a black rock at the foot of Kurkar's throne, and his brains are dashed across the bottom of Kurkar's robe. As he intended, Gesar's inconceivable strength undermines the demon's confidence in the strength he understands. The people of Hor are dismayed and, not knowing what to do, they return to their homes in an unsettled silence. What began as a happy day, has ended badly.

When Kurkar tells Sechan Dugmo what has happened, she is filled with fear, and knows that the smith's apprentice can be no other than Gesar, and that if the Kingdom of Hor is to remain, he must be destroyed.

She fully knows the extent of his cleverness and his power, and she tells Kurkar that a ruse must be devised to undo him. Kurkar, although he is reluctant to lose the boy's beguiling artistry, senses that there may be some truth in what she is telling him, and so next morning he summons the young smith.

He favors the boy with one of his most pleasant smiles, and the air around Gesar is filled with a confiding warmth. "There is a huge red tiger beyond the mountains to the north of my palace. He troubles my people there, and I would like you, since you are both clever and strong, to capture the beast so that it may be chained here in my throne room." Gesar pretends that he is too young, too weak, too fearful; but at each objection, Kurkar smiles and assures him, until at last he agrees to go.

In the weeks of Gesar's absence, things seem to go easily in the Kingdom of Hor, and just when Kurkar and Sechan Dugmo are beginning to feel that the disturbances that have bothered them have ended, the smith's apprentice returns, leading a huge tiger at the end of an iron chain. He attaches the chain to a peg in the throne room, and none, not even Kurkar himself or his two brothers, now dare enter there for fear of the raging beast. "He is hungry, and will not be calm until he is fed," the boy explains. "But because he has become used to human flesh, he will eat nothing else." The thought of sacrificing one of his subjects to feed his new pet disturbs Kurkar, but before he can consider his dilemma, the tiger pulls free and pounces on the prime minister of Hor, ripping him to pieces, eating his flesh and drinking his blood. "Take him back! Get him out of here!" the demon king cries. And the boy removes the sated beast and takes him back to his distant homeland.

Now Kurkar's sense of certainty has been undermined, and the atmosphere in Hor has become strange and uncertain. So now Gesar begins in earnest the destruction of the demons of the East. He appears before the king in the guise of an Indian magician, and tells Kurkar that all these misfortunes will be resolved if the great piece of meteoric iron, which fell as a celestial blessing upon Hor and is kept in the palace stronghold, is forged into a great chain. This chain must be fixed to the top of the palace gate, and someone must climb up and remove the head of Gesar's brother warrior that hangs there. The head must be removed, because it attracts evil influences, and buried with all honors. Before this errand can be accomplished, he, the great magician, must bless Kurkar and all his subjects by placing his hat on each of their heads. Then will Hor become strong and peaceful once again.

So on the next day, the anxious king and all his subjects line up, and one by one, they let the magician touch his greasy pointed black hat to their heads. And one by one they become overwhelmed by a kind of languorous stupor. In such a state of mind, Kurkar calls for Gesar, who has now resumed the form of the apprentice smith, gives him the sacred bar of meteoric iron, and tells him what he wishes to be done.

Within three days, the great chain is made. Many warriors of

Hor, one by one, try, by scaling the palace walls, to lift it to the summit of the gate. And all who try, crash to the ground and are killed. Kurkar and his brothers and his court watch the spectacle in paralyzed horror, and it only ends when the apprentice smith climbs up the wall, as easily as a monkey, fixes the chain, and slides back down to the ground, carrying the head of his former friend. Kurkar and Sechan Dugmo yearn for this nightmare to end, as they watch the king's palace guard take the head off into the mountains to be buried. But a week later, a battered messenger comes to the silver palace, and tells the king that his guard, one and all, have been buried in a landslide as they were burying the severed head, and Kurkar's palace is filled with a miasma of indecision and a fear of inevitable doom.

During that very night, Gesar, disguised as all three of the ancestral gods of Hor, comes in a dream to Kurkar. "Tomorrow morning, send your wife, Sechan Dugmo, and your two brothers, Kurser and Kurnag, to the great mountain peak to the south, along with all your priests, your troops and your subjects. There they will see a great miracle. They will see the sacred dance of our retinue, which no living being has ever seen before. The blessings for the people of Hor will be immeasurable. While they watch, you must remain here in this palace alone, and pray without ceasing to the power of your gods. Only in this way will Hor be preserved." And the very next morning, Kurkar gives the command. Everyone in Hor goes to the mountain peak in the south, and he remains in his palace by himself.

As the sun rises at the mountain peak, at a place called Tsara Padma Togden, seven enormous gleaming white spiders move slowly across the rocks and transform themselves into seven dancing male deities. They move in the most graceful and original swirls and turns. Neither monk, nor layman, nor lord, nor servant has ever seen such agility and suppleness, nor such beauty of costume and form. The magnificent costumes of the celestial dancers change with each new movement in the dance. And the performers, never showing any fatigue, dance continuously and without interruption. Kurser is entranced by this amazing display, and Kurnag, by the deities' evident power. The people of Hor, utterly spellbound, watch them and lose all knowledge of time. As if they had been completely transported to another realm, they lose all sense of time and place.

Left alone, Kurkar, King of Hor, cannot focus his mind or settle in any one place. He roves restlessly through the palace for the whole day, and such prayers as he can brokenly mumble seem like barren echoes. At last night comes, and still alone, he falls asleep. A dazzling white light immediately envelops the palace, and Kurkar, waking with a start, sees Gesar standing before him, shining like the sun in his golden armor and holding in his hand his sword of meteoric iron.

"Do you know me, Kurkar, Demon Lord? I am Gesar, King of Ling. It is my country you have stolen, my wife you have married, my friends you have killed, my subjects you have enslaved, and my possessions you now enjoy. I am here to take back my own."

"Ah," cries Kurkar, his eyes bulging with terrified understanding, "how blind I have been not to know you were here!"

Gesar does not give him time to say another word, but he forces the bridle into his mouth and puts the saddle on his back, and crushes him to the floor. Then with a single sword blow, cutting through the air like a scythe come to harvest the world, he cuts off Kurkar's head, which rolls into the middle of the room. He then dissolves the demon's being into the empty sky of sunrise.

At dawn the next day, all the people of Hor still watch the dance of the gods, unaware that any time at all has passed. A day and night have gone by without their knowing, and during that time, in response to Gesar's call, all the forces of Ling have gathered on every side around the people of Hor. Riding on the horse of wonder and power, Kyang Go Karkar, Gesar in full array rides to the summit of the sky. From there, he sends down a cascade of thunder arrows, killing the demon lord Kurser, sending an arrow through his bronze shield marked with a boar, even as he stands stupefied and sated by the dance of the illusory deities. From every side, the warriors of Ling attack, and all who resist are slaughtered on the spot.

Many surrender, and Gesar makes them swear loyalty to him, and sends them back to Hor. Only Kurnag, the black demon of anger, seeing that the forces against him are too great, manages to escape despite the troops that chase after him. The heads of the Sakyapa are said to keep this demon and his few attendants in a rock prison to this very day.

Gesar calls for Sechan Dugmo. She is stunned and shaken, uncertain whether she has just woken from a dream or simply passed from one nightmare into another. He sends her back to Ling. Gesar himself stays behind, for he must kill the child who is Sechan Dugmo's son by Kurkar. The three-year-old boy has a mortal hatred of Gesar and dreams only of exterminating him when he grows up. The boy's resolve is unshakable, and Gesar arranges for a boulder to fall from a mountain pass where the boy is hiding, and he is crushed to death. Having done this painful deed, Gesar returns at last to Ling.

3

The warriors of Ling are overjoyed at their victory and at their king's return. They set out a great feast, while the dancers perform a dance called, "The Tiger Feasts." Sechan Dugmo, alone in her tent and still wearing the clothes of a queen of Hor, is by turns bitter, ashamed, grief-stricken and afraid to show herself to the people of Ling. So Gesar comes to visit her in her tent, but she cannot bear to look at him, and she hides in the shadows. Standing in the tent, wearing his splendid armor, Gesar speaks to her softly:

Sechan Dugmo, queen and wife,
Remorse at what each of us has done,
Anger at what each of us has seen the other do,
Sorrow that true love has proved so fragile,
Sadness that passing love has been compelling and disastrous,
Doubt that even genuine love can be restored,
Fear that neither decency nor joy have a place
In such deceitful and dangerous terrain,
All these things, O dear companion of my heart,
Seem to separate us so, and yet,
We share them utterly.

With that, Gesar walks quietly from the tent.

The next morning, when all the warriors and subjects of Ling have assembled before the palace, Sechan Dugmo presents herself in her native dress to Gesar. She is placed to his left and Todong, pale and now almost skinny after his sojourn in prison, is stationed to Gesar's right. Though there is much joy and cheering, there is also a somber undertone of uncertainty. Then Gesar calls on Todong to explain his actions and to tell what lesson he has learned in prison. And Todong, with expressions ranging from arrogance to aggrieved piteousness, sings this song:

Though I have been blessed with cleverness and strength
Because of many past lifetimes of good actions,

I am still just an ordinary human being.
Though I have been blessed with high standing and honor,
Still I am just a mortal human being.
Even though what I have done seemed reasonable,
Things have not worked out.
Now, for three years I have ended up in prison,
Completely alone, and you want to know what I have found.
Well, my young king, you will not be pleased.
Well, my timid subjects, you will not be satisfied.

Dwelling for years in a dark grimy hole,
The events of my life have swarmed before my eyes.
Over and over, I have played out all my possibilities.
From this, I can say that I can find no reason
For why things are the way they are
Or why they are not different.
I can find no reason for why I am the way I am
Or how I could possibly be different.

I have not chosen what I am,
And I have not chosen a single one
Of the hail of many thoughts that teem in my brain.
Even in this hovel of a prison, awake or asleep,
Thoughts of obliging women, faithful servants,
Obedient armies and endless conquests of all kinds
Offer themselves to me so vividly,
With all their trappings of brocade, fine horses, gems,
Soft cushions and music.
Oh, an infinity of detailed delight. I must have them;
I was always like this and I still am.
Who is human who does not want such things?

There is no existence apart from that.
Dreadful insults, humiliations, losses,
Cruel tortures and hideous deaths,
All of them race through my mind, cutting me deep.
Who would not plot revenge and plan escapes?

Oh, you may wish me to be other than I am,
And even I may wish it,
But alone in the dark, I have seen
That I am born a human being
And will not depart from schemes
To obtain the good things of this world,
And to avoid its many evil pains.
If you would blame me,
Say that you are otherwise.
If you think I should be different,
Kill me and let me find a life in some other kind of realm.
But if you are honest,
Even if you hate me,
You will simply let me be.

Many were convinced by Todong's song. Some had contempt,
and some snickered, but none could think of a way to refute it,
and finally all fell silent. Then Gesar sang a song in reply:

There is no one in the world
Who can exceed Todong at strategy.
When it comes to calculating
Gain and loss, he is the master.
But because he thinks only of himself,
He can never win.

The great queen, Sechan Dugmo,
Is the kindest of beings.
No one in this world is more gentle and loving,
More protective and proud of her people and mate.
But without an object for her devotion,
Despite her best efforts, she becomes confused
And ends by betraying everything she loves.

In all the realms of existence, it is always this way:
If you seek for yourself, you will lose your self;
If you seek for another, you will lose your world.
Existence cannot be confirmed by existence.

The luminous magic of reality,
The joyful power of life, is so
Only in its own reference.

Dear friends, when a raindrop falls into a still pond,
It dissolves inseparably in its own nature,
And nothing has occurred.
But when the same raindrop falls into the same pond,
Ripples shine and dance on the water's skin.
From these two ways of seeing one thing
Comes the true magic that raises and destroys kingdoms,
That increases joy or misery, brilliance or degradation.

From just this moment at the heart of life,
The demon lords of Hor wove a shiny iron net
Of sticky obsessive thoughts.
In this way, they created an illusory realm
Where phantom selves race after shimmering hallucinations.

Though we have subjugated these demons,
Their legacy always returns and must be cut continually.

Dear friends, please look and see:
The ceaseless fire of cosmic love,
The vast and mysterious realm of unknowing,
The unstoppable wind of cosmic anger,
All are the spontaneous expressions of inseparable union.
They are the great pulse that radiates and binds the forms of life.
These are the self-existing power of liberation,
As their vivid movement consumes the private dramas of individuality.
Whether we struggle or rejoice, this is so.

But the red demon Kurkar
Has drawn from the heat of unconditional love
The thread of selfish craving.

Dear friends, please look and see:
What is seen and who sees it exist only as light.
What is heard and who hears it exist only as sound.
What is touched and who touches it exist only as feeling.
What is smelled and who smells it exist only as scent.
What is known and who knows it exist only as consciousness.
What is called self and what is called other cannot be divided,
But have no other existence.
Body and world are inseparable.
Whether we struggle or rejoice, this is so.

But the pale demon Kurser
Has drawn from the limitless expanse of perception
The thread of confused possessive self-absorption.

Dear friends, please look and see:
All forms of experience, of feeling, of knowing,
Are never separate from ever-present naked awareness.
Awareness cannot be bound and does not come or go.
It is like the cosmic mirror where all reflections arise.
Because awareness rests only in itself, there is peace.
Whether we struggle or rejoice, this is so.

But the black demon Kurnag
Has drawn from this uncompromising completion
The thread of defensive fury.
If we wish to uncover
What is genuine and good in this life,
Continually and moment by moment
We must cut through the net of deception
Of possessing and being possessed.

If we wish to see
The source of fearlessness that opens every instant,
We must abandon our struggle
To possess and be possessed,
On the spot.

If we wish for ourselves and future generations
That the innate goodness of human dignity
Be the confidence of our life together,
Then, continually, we must renew our allegiance
To the brilliance shining eternally before us.

The world is healed or harmed each instant
In the stillness of our hearts.
Whether we struggle or rejoice, this is so.

People of Ling, this is our power and the power of all.
We must open the true kingdom in our hearts.

Then Gesar, the great Tiger Lord shows the people of Ling how to practice the discipline that relies on the innate power of mind. Sechan Dugmo, the lords, warriors and subjects of Ling, even Todong, at least for the time that he continues in this discipline, take this teaching to heart. In this way, the Kingdom of Ling is restored.

PART V

1

To the west, where the land seems perpetually tinged with the red of the setting sun, lies the demon Kingdom of Jang. For many years, Satham, King of Jang, has reigned there in somnolent satiety, utterly absorbed like a god in contemplating the beauties of his domain. But with his marriage to his second wife, he has become increasingly restless, agitated and rapacious. His extravagant passion for his new queen must be celebrated in luxuries large and small, rare foods, music, bombastic speech and lavish displays. He commands palaces to be built on peaks that give a pleasing view. He orders his armies to march in review, so that his bride will admire his increasing power, and he begins to dream of conquering all the neighboring lands and establishing an empire that will last through time. He dreams that the ancestral deities of his domain, all floating on multicolored clouds—one riding a bay horse and wearing a moon-colored coat of mail, one riding on a black yak and wearing armor of iron, and one riding a speckled goat and wearing armor of lightning—come to him and sing a great song of promise:

O Satham, King of Jang, you can be as we are:
Boundless as desire, enduring as earth,
And free as the sudden wind.

O Satham, King of Jang, you can live as we do:
In a delirious bliss that has never ceased
And has never been touched by fear.

O Satham, King of Jang, you must feast as we do:
Drink the sap of life, the delicious essence,
And join with us.
Conquer the lands around you—
Destroy Gesar, and take Ling.
Drink from this golden pool of strength.
Join with us in eternity, O brother king.

This dream and the plans that rise from it alarm his prime minister, Petul Kalon, who fears that they will stir the hostility of the fearsome Gesar of Ling. But Satham, King of Jang, will not be deterred by the wise counsel of his faithful friend, and he presses forward with his projects.

Far away in Ling, standing on his palace roof, Gesar suddenly sees all that takes place in the land of Jang. He sees King Satham, burning like an ember on his throne, eager to consume the world in an eternity of bliss. He sees that love and portents goad him on in a mad race for eternity which will transform the entire earth into his demented paradise. The demon lord has fixed his mind on bending the physical world to the shape of his desire, and this has made his body invulnerable to direct assault. Gesar sees that Satham must be stopped or the new-won peace of Ling will soon be overwhelmed, as the elements themselves are disrupted and thrown into chaos. But it is not on the strength of his body that Gesar must rely; it is on the power of the mind of confidence.

In the center of Satham's palace is a walled-in garden that surrounds a small stone temple. Within this temple is the statue of a horse, carved from an enormous conch that embodies the protection of the demon kings of Jang. The very morning following Satham's dream, a palace servant sees that three white mules have miraculously appeared in the doorless enclosure surrounding the temple and are peacefully grazing on the yellow flowers there. He summons Satham, who comes accompanied by his bride, from whom he is inseparable. Together they gape at the strange spectacle, but the bride, unable to see as clearly as she would like, leans out over the wall, loses her balance and falls to her death in the garden.

Shocked and distraught, Satham orders the wall torn down, and he carries the body of his beloved wife to the throne room. He cradles her in his arms and will not put her down or let anyone enter. He forbids anyone to speak of her death or to mention anyone else's death. It becomes the law of the land that no funeral may take place. When he hears that the three white mules that appeared in the temple garden have dissolved into the sky as a white rainbow, he knows that it is Gesar who created the illusion that killed his wife, and he orders from his locked throne room that the war with Ling go forward. He has the conch statue destroyed for the part it has inadvertently played in Gesar's lethal deception. Vowing that the dominon of his love will never cease, Satham sends forth his troops under his son's command.

On the first night when he has ventured out of his homeland, the Prince of Jang dreams that he sees an imposing warrior riding on a blazing red horse, and the next morning, while his army still sleeps, the prince rides out to scout the countryside. When he encounters exactly such a man as he just dreamed of, riding exactly such a horse, somehow he is not surprised. He feels, in fact, overjoyed, as if he were meeting his father again after a long absence. The warrior smiles at him, and suddenly, when he has drawn close, strikes him on the forehead with the butt of his whip. The prince falls unconscious from his horse, and when he wakes, he finds the warrior staring down at him. "Do you not know me?" he asks. And the prince's heart is flooded with a brilliant light of relief and joy. His mind is cleared of the grandiose craving and desperate paranoia of his father's domain, and he sings out:

> The vermilion light of boundless longing,
> The long gold rays of sun's suggestion
> That trail over earth's edge at the end of day,
> The glowing purple of towering sky palaces
> Burned, dissolved, unshadowed
> In the shadeless noon of Gesar's impartial blaze,
> Are revealed as none other than this ever-wakeful heart.
> In seeing you, I meet myself at last.

He recognizes Gesar of Ling's true nature as his own and vows that there will never be any opposition between them.

Gesar, riding on the powerful back of the miracle horse, Kyang Go Karkar, flies by himself into the heartland of Jang. He alights near the palace, on the edge of the sacred lake there. He transforms Kyang Go Karkar into a tree, his saddle into a large puddle, his helmet, armor and clothing into flowers growing at the water's edge, and he himself into a tiny iron bee with razor-sharp wings.

On hearing of his son's disappearance, Satham knows that Gesar's magic is once again the cause, and that he alone must lead the armies of Jang if they are to prevail. Because he has completely identified himself with his ancestral deities and they with him, Satham's body is impenetrable and cannot be pierced or harmed by anything from the outside; but if he is to be invulnerable to any inner illness or decay, he must drink the water of life, which a goddess in the sacred lake is sworn to give him. So, after kissing and caressing her rotting form, he sets the corpse of his beloved wife upon his throne and goes out to the lakeside. There he calls upon the water goddess. He feels great relief as he sees her, small and delicate, trailing wisps of perfumed mist, floating toward him. He reaches his hands to take the water that she pours out from her golden vase, but before he can swallow a drop, the iron bee flies into his mouth and down his throat.

There Gesar flies furiously through his innards, slashing with his iron wings at stomach, intestines and blood vessels, cutting them to ribbons. Satham, screaming in agony as he is attacked from within, hacks at his own body with his sword in a vain effort to kill his tormentor from outside. Finally Gesar pierces the demon's heart and chops it to pieces, and Satham of Jang, blood pouring out from his ears, nose and mouth, dies.

Though he may have been opposed to his lord's extravagant and rash plans, the Prime Minister of Jang is horrified at the spectacle of Satham's hideous demise and knows that it is indeed Gesar's doing. He realizes that Gesar has somehow invaded the body of the king, and so before he can escape, the prime minister plugs up all the corpse's orifices with butter and places it on the cremation pyre. However, as the flames lick the corpse's skin, Gesar transforms himself into a tiny red fly and he transforms Satham's consciousness into a minute black fly, and they escape through the tiny aperture at the crown of the corpse's head. Gesar then dissolves the consciousness of Satham into space, and in his

109

own form, he rejoins and leads his army.

The warriors of Ling sweep across the land without opposition until they meet with the great hordes of Jang encamped beside a poison lake. The two armies join in battle beneath flights of arrows so dense that the sun is darkened. The hooves of many thousand steeds stamping, charging and wheeling, raise a cloud of dust so black, that the only light is that which flickers on shields and armor and flashes from the blades of swirling swords and spear tips. The rattle of arrows, the clash of arms and the crush of men and beasts are deafening as ceaseless thunder. The battle resembles a roiling thunderstorm tearing up the earth. Ten thousand of the warriors of Jang fall, while the army of Ling loses but a hundred men. The army of Jang falls back in panic and confusion from the wild onslaught, and runs headlong before its furious pursuers.

Amongst all the warriors of Jang, only one will not give ground, and he hurls out his defiance as he stands alone with his bloody sword beside the black water of the poison lake, amid a heap of slain and broken warriors of Ling. This is none other than Petul, Prime Minister of Jang, who after his master's death now leads his armies. In so doing, and despite his previous doubts, he has assumed the powers and aims of his gods and race. So Gesar, mounted on his wonder steed, leaps into the sky. A rainbow circles his head, and his jeweled armor burns as a living flame. From Kyang Go Karkar, yellow tongues of fire and black plumes of smoke billow into the sky. But even at this sight, the Prime Minister of Jang does not weaken, and he cries out:

Gesar, evil magician of the people of Ling,
I know you for what you are:
Destroyer of light and destroyer of bliss,
You are the great sorrow and dark void at the end of life.

Though my lord was rash,
His passion was vast and splendid.
Though my lord was extravagant,
His vision was of an incomparable beauty.
To be in his noble presence
Was to experience inspiration and joy,
Was to be far from the laborious degradation
Of your ordinary world.
Though he is dead, his wife also dead,
His son vanished, all by your design,
The power of his splendor lives in my body
And the dreams of his gods live in my heart.
I am eternal as light.
I have gone far beyond your strength.
Today, you will boil in this poison lake.

Gesar and Petul shoot arrow after arrow at each other, but as each shoots, the other dodges, until both their quivers are empty and they throw aside their useless bows. Then Gesar dismounts from his horse and the two warriors fight with swords, slashing and parrying, all the while shouting and cursing at each other. Finally, by a great effort, Petul begins to drive Gesar to the edge of the lake, and there the two begin hand-to-hand combat. And for all his divine power, Gesar, for the first time in his life, feels his strength begin to ebb.

All at once, Kyang Go Karkar, seeing his master's desperate plight, flies over Petul and snares his upraised arm in one of the stirrups. He hoists the struggling minister high up into the sky and drops him into the center of the black poison lake, which foams and boils as it strips the flesh from his bones.

Their conquest of Jang secure, Gesar returns wearily with his men to their encampment, and there they sleep through the night, too tired even to eat or light a fire.

The next morning, Gesar, in his most splendid armor, and seated on Kyang Go Karkar, has the Prince of Jang brought before him and commands him to rule that land on his behalf. Then horse and rider fly up into the blue cloudless sky, where they seem to fuse and became an enormous golden garuda, floating on immense vulture-like wings in the center of the sky, and to a lilting melody, they sing this song:

Not relying on anything,
Not prolonging anything,
Not hastening anything to its end:
Here the dramas of life swell and resolve without imprint
As a rainbow pulsing in the sky.
The great tides of experience shimmer
As the tints of color in this arc of light.
On such magical sky bridges do men,
Demons, and gods wander and play out
Their poignant deeds of hope and fear.

I, Gesar, the self-born Garuda,
Fly through the pure air of a cool sky,
Open beyond measurement or memory,
And its bright crystal winds pour directly
Through the chambers of my heart.

So, though joyful, the warriors of Ling find the memory of this song haunting as they return home to the Kingdom of Ling.

2

A week of feasting follows on this swift victory over the demon lord of Jang. The dancers perform the dance called, "The Gods Fall from the Garuda's Beak." It is both a relief and a joy to the nobles, warriors and people of Ling that their kingdom is not only restored, but again powerful, and that their king, Gesar, is an abiding inspiration for their confidence. On the evening that marks the end of this period of celebration, Gesar stands smiling amid the flickering firelight, and makes a vow:

The rhythm of breath pervading the world
Reveals the separation of self and other as unborn,
And the bias toward inner or outer experience as unknown.
This is the synchronization of body and mind.

Resolve the restless torments of demonic anxiety
In the fearless heart-space of nonthought,
And you will find peace in the natural state.

In every breath, absorb into your being all the terrors of this earth;
Radiate like a sun the light of unconditional confidence,
And the true dignity of this world will always be restored.

Singing thus, Gesar then tells the people of Ling of his vow to practice this in seclusion for the next thirteen years. He encourages them to do likewise, as much as their lives will permit, and the next morning, he withdraws to his shrine room and seals the doors.

Part VI

1

At the end of ten years of solitary retreat, the goddess Manene rises up to Gesar out of the reflection of the noonday sun in a bowl of water on the window sill. She sits easily on a flower floating in the bowl and sings to him:

O Great Dragon Lord, you slumber
Like a spangled monster in a cave
While Shingti, the great yellow demon of the South,
Gains daily in power and influence.
He must be conquered now or it will be too late.

But Gesar replies that three years remain before his vow will be fulfilled, and he will march on King Shingti then. He has lived his life in accordance with his vows; they are one with his being, and so to break his retreat will surely cause misfortune for him in this and other lives, as well as trouble for the people of Ling. But Manene insists:

There is no doubt that the time is now
For the destruction of Shingti;
Otherwise, great evil will soon infect the earth.

Padma Sambhava's wish and your own nature
Make your action here inevitable.
You know I have never wished you any harm,
But thoughts of individual good or ill
Have no place in determining your being.
Your vow is not to words and deeds,
It is to wakefulness and confidence itself.
You must act, and now. Do not doubt it.

And without another word, clapping her hands, she vanishes.

When Manene disappears, Gesar calls Sechan Dugmo. She is astonished to hear that he is ending his retreat and weeps in fear for his health and for the well-being of Ling altogether. Gesar holds her tenderly.

"Dearest friend of my life, if the path that purifies the human realm of demonic possession and establishes the way of genuine goodness is to be open to all people, I must immediately conquer the demons of the South. If I have never feared the alternation between life and death, how can I now hold back for any personal reason whatsoever?" And so saying, Gesar calls for the warriors of Ling, Hor and Jang to assemble within the week before his palace.

Everyone is shocked that Gesar is suddenly ending his retreat, but when Sechan Dugmo explains his reasons, all agree. The warriors of Ling are also deeply disturbed that the armies of their recent enemies are to be a part of the expedition. However when Gesar appears before them in his golden battle armor, which sparkles and gleams in the sun as Kyang Go Karkar prances joyfully, he tells them sternly that the armies must join as one if the kingdom is to be as one. And he warns them that any thought of jealousy or distrust, any thought of separation or superiority, will compromise their success.

"Shingti is a powerful, crude and brutal demon," Gesar continues. "He is sustained neither by ancestral gods nor talismans, nor beliefs of any sort. He does not even have a government, for he needs only an army. He is sustained simply by his own relentless accumulation, by what he has heaped up for himself and his people in the past, and by the ape-like intensity of his continuous grasping. But if we are utterly united, we will be too great for even his huge mouth to swallow." And so, within a week of Manene's visit, the armies of Ling, Hor and Jang have set out and are encamped before the iron bridge that borders on the dusty yellow earth of King Shingti's realm.

The massed armies, practicing their maneuvers on the riverbank with thousands of red, gold and silver pennants, resemble a turbulent sea of dancing flames. The guards of the bridge are surprised to see this immense army encamped there on the far side of the stream, covering the entire plain. They do not know whether these are friends or foe, so they send messengers to King Shingti for instructions.

The messengers find the demon king sprawled on his throne, seated on a bloodstained human skin, and after having offered him some furs, they tell him about the army across the river.

"I don't know anything about it, but whoever they are, they should know that the plain where they are presuming to take their ease is land that I have long laid claim to, and if they want to stay there another minute, they will have to pay good rent. Otherwise, I'll smash them to bits and grind their bones to dust. Find out who they are and tell them that." The messengers return to the bridge, and call to the troops across the water, conveying the king's message. On Gesar's instruction, the soldiers invite King Shingti's messengers to visit them and discuss the matter, and the messengers, once assured of their safe conduct, enter Gesar's camp. There they boldly proclaim King Shingti's demands and threats.

"Thank you for the message you have brought, my friends, and I salute your courage for coming before me," Gesar tells them with easy assurance. "But I must tell you that I, Gesar of Ling, conqueror of the demons of the North, East, and West, will stay in this place for as long as it suits me, whether that be a day or a year. This land is not King Shingti's, and so there is no question of obligation to him. Neither your master nor his army are my equal, so there is nothing to fear on that account.

"However, I have come with quite a different aim. My uncle, Todong, most respected and admired amongst the elder warriors of Ling and a man of great stature, wisdom and wealth, has a son twenty years old. And once every year for the past twelve years, I have had a dream that Todong's son, who is, in a manner of speaking, my nephew, will marry the daughter of your king. King Shingti's daughter, Metok Lhadze, is now fifteen years old if I am not mistaken, and it is time for her to wed. If your lord gives us his daughter willingly, then we will shower him with gold and silver. But if he refuses, then I shall lay waste to his domain and carry off his daughter anyhow. The choice is his."

"The daughter of King Shingti is his only child. She will inherit all that is his and will succeed him on the Southern throne," replies the braver of the messengers. "Do you think he will send her to a land of shepherds and nomads? He will consider your request most impudent and will surely massacre you, each and every one. But we will take him your message, as you wish, and we will see what will come of it."

The messengers display far less bravado in their report to King Shingti. They tell the demon lord of the size and power of Gesar's army, of the king of Ling's immovable confidence, and they suggest that perhaps it might indeed be best if Metok Lhadze were married to Todong's son. King Shingti screams with rage and, gnashing his coal black teeth, stands up on his bloody throne. He pulls two long golden whips from his belt, and with arms as big around as tree trunks, he whips the messengers, flaying them alive before his troops. Then, in a voice with the sound of a trumpet, he declaims:

There is only one infallible law of life,
And he who does not know it is, in fact, already dead.
There are only two kinds of things:
What is mine and what is not.
And everyone knows that if one increases,
The other must decline.
If I see a field, surely it is mine.
If I hear a name, whoever bears it is mine.
There is no pleasure or pain that is not in my domain,
Nor thought, nor dream, nor any possibility.

You, my subjects, have profited,
Living according to this law.
If we do not devour this wretched upstart,
Whatever he may say, he will devour us,
And we will be forced from the fortresses we have gained
To enter an endless realm of hopeless loss.

Then, after sending half his army to attack the armies of Ling and ordering the others to defend the castle stronghold, he retires angrily to his private rooms.

That night, Metok Lhadze has a terrible dream. She sees her father's skin stretched across the ground of his land by four large spears through his hands and feet. On the piece of ground where

119

his stomach would be, there is his castle, collapsing in a tornado of fire as blood belches out of its windows and doors. She wakes in terror and runs to tell her father who, though awake, is still in bed. His mood changes from indulgence to rage as he listens to her, and he strikes her across the mouth and orders the guards to lock her in her room, high up in a tower of the citadel, until the war is at an end.

But that same night, Gesar dreams of a tiny mounted warrior in silver armor with white pennants on his helmet, urging him on. So before it is light, the Lord of Ling sends half his men upstream to ford the river, and he himself leads the other half across the iron bridge. His two armies crush the defenders between them, so later when the main body of the southern demon's army arrives at mid-day, they are already outflanked.

The battle is terrible indeed. The warriors fight with arrows, swords and spears; while the shepherds of Ling, skilled in throwing the lasso, catch their enemies from a distance, jerk them from their saddles, and drag them along the ground beneath the horses' hooves. The army of King Shingti is massacred and all the generals who led it are decapitated. Their corpses are cast into a mass grave and burned.

When King Shingti, striding back and forth on his castle's parapet, anxious at hearing no report from his forces, sees the great oily column of black smoke, he is uncertain whether it indicates victory or defeat, so he sends out all but his palace guard. If his troops have won, then it will make no difference, but if they have lost, then this new fresh army may catch Gesar's tired warriors by surprise. This second army meets with the same fate as the first, and is utterly destroyed. But the great towering coil of smoke from the second pyre is invisible to King Shingti in the night.

Early the next morning, as the sun is about to rise, King Shingti is awakened from an uneasy sleep by a strange commotion. Gesar has once again raced with his army through the night, and taking up positions all around the citadel, has set fire to the walls in the four cardinal directions. Shingti sees that his proud kingdom has become a burning hell and he is surrounded on all sides by walls of flame. Then he hears a terrible crack, loud as if the earth and sky were parting. He turns and sees that the great column of turquoise that is the long-life pole of his realm, and that extended from the foundations of his castle to its summit, has fractured from the heat into a hundred pieces. But he has, since childhood, developed a method to escape from just such circumstances: he has forged a magic ladder on which he can climb up to the clouds in the sky. Swiftly, he runs to the roof and unrolls the ladder. He hurls it high into the clouds and is madly climbing up when Gesar sees him.

Gesar and the miracle horse, Kyang Go Karkar, are transformed into a turquoise dragon with obsidian eyes and fly high into the smoky sky. The dragon dances through the coils of smoke, and with a flash of his talons of meteoric iron, he severs the ladder's golden cords. King Shingti, screaming and cursing as he falls, comes crashing to earth. Gesar, now as a golden dragon with ruby eyes, dives into the fire, dancing with the flames; and before the demon lord is quite dead, flays the skin off his body and pins it to the ground with four spears. "The skin of this demon, when dry, will provide a powerful medicine that is both antidote and protection for you," he shouts to his astonished warriors.

As for Metok Lhadze, she is trapped in the tower of the burning citadel, running from window to window in a desperate search for escape. Gesar sees her leaning out of one of the windows and he calls up to her: "If you are at heart a demoness, throw yourself out and fall into the flames. If you are of a noble race, come to me through the air." The young girl, without another thought, throws herself into the black hellish void and, floating high above

121

the blazing city, drops down, light as a leaf, into the great Lord's arms. At first she thinks that she has landed in the coils of a great shiny black dragon with golden eyes, but then she sees that she is seated on King Gesar's lap as he rides across the ruined city on his great horse, Kyang Go Karkar.

2

The war is then ended, and all of King Shingti's treasures, hidden in a vault beneath the mountains, become the property of Ling. On his return home, Gesar gives the young princess in marriage to Todong's son, and all celebrate a great victory banquet. The dancers perform a dance called, "The Relative and the Absolute Do Not Part." Late in the night, Gesar, who seems quite drunk, sings this slow song:

When the steel sword
Sweeps through the cold air,
Thought is nonthought.

When the little princess, Metok Lhadze,
Jumps into the burning air,
Thought is nonthought.

When I sit down
On the golden throne of Ling,
Thought is nonthought.

When there is proper respect,
When there is loyalty,

When there is discipline in body, speech and mind,
And all actions are for the good of all,
Thought is nonthought.

When a warrior displays the four kinds of elegance,
The four demon lords are spontaneously destroyed
And the goodness of this world is bright as a new sun,
Because thought is nonthought.

When, my dear brother warriors,
Actions are not based on pain, and there are no calculations
Concerning temporary advantages and future goals;
When, in short, you stop trying to escape this world as it is,
Well, then there is nothing to worry about,
But there is always plenty to do.

The presence of wisdom
Is not the precondition of action or its result;
It arises freely and constantly
As the impeccable warrior
Dances with seeming necessity.
It is neither thought nor nonthought.

Great beings of Ling,
You have been splendid, courageous,
Generous and kind.
By your conduct, you have changed the world.
Thank you all so very much.

And with that, Gesar, the Dragon Lord, rises to return to his tent. He stumbles slightly as he descends from his throne. Sechan Dugmo moves to take his arm, and some of the warriors worry and others smile, but seeing the great hero as a human being, joy and sadness mingle in their hearts.

PART VII

1

E arly one morning, in the crisp clear light of dawn while Gesar and the people of Ling still sleep, Sechan Dugmo wakes and walks up into the foothills of the mountains. There she sings this spontaneous song, called "The Rainbow Palace of Pure Presence," to the purity of the four directions, which now, after all Gesar's battles, has been restored.

i

In the world
That is and is not this world,

In the bliss
That pervades and does not pervade this world,

In the unfabricated instant
That is and is not this,

You, O Sun, are the pure light that has never known darkness.
You are the origin of all movements and cycles and do not move.

You are ever the enduring center of the centerless,
The light indivisible from all light.

ii

Gleaming in a rainbow circle, unsought and unseen,
You, O Light of East, appearing as all the kinds of blue,
Appearing as water and cold,
Untouched by the anger of obscuration;
You are the clarity of all light.

Gleaming in a rainbow circle, unsought and unseen
You, O Light of West, appearing as all kinds of red,
Enticing and appearing as fire,
Nothing has ever been separated from you;
You are the joy of light.

Gleaming in a rainbow circle, unsought and unseen,
You, O Light of the South, appearing as all kinds of yellow,
Sufficient and appearing as earth,
Untouched by any kind of neediness or want;
You are the panoply of light.

Gleaming in a rainbow circle, unsought and unseen,
You, O Light of the North, appearing as all kinds of black,
Complete and appearing as wind and motion,
Nothing can stand against you;
You are the action of light.

iii

There is neither raft,
Nor wreckage, nor destination, nor rescue
In the vast and shimmering trackless seas
Of your deathless *amrita* mind.

Whether appearing as element or deity or light,
You consume the ocean of senses
As spontaneous offerings into your own nature.

Whether as element or deity or light,
You consume the clouds of mental events
As spontaneous offerings into your own bliss.

Whether as element or deity or light,
You consume the lightning of insight
As offerings into your own radiance.

Whether as element or deity or light,
You consume the thunder of duality
As the offerings of union in your pure expanse.

Whether as element, deity, light or vow,
You leave behind nothing,
Even silence,
Even suchness itself.

Then, happily, she walks down the hill and smiles as she sees in
the distance smoke rising from the tents of the people of Ling, who
are awake and now light their fires to prepare the morning meal.

2

One month later, all the affairs of Ling have been set in order and Gesar announces that the time has come for him to finish his retreat and that all who wish to join him may do so. Accordingly, he, Sechan Dugmo, and many nobles and warriors of Ling and their families journey eastward until they reach a rocky milk-white mountain so high that its peak reaches beyond the pale blue summit of the sky.

At first light on the morning following their arrival, Gesar takes his seat. To his right sit his ministers on tiger-skin seats and to his left, his queen and the ladies of the court on leopard-skin seats, and before him, on bear-skin seats, are his generals and warriors. The very sight of them is like the words of an ancient song come to life.

In the center sits Gesar of Ling on his golden lion throne.
He is warriorship itself and is arrayed like a Rigden king.
His golden armor radiates the light of the sun.
His chain-mail glitters like stars in the sky.
His gold helmet, adorned with fluttering white pennants,
Blazes like the sun.
His silver shield shines like the moon.
He wears a tiger-skin quiver, and his arrows are lightning itself.
His leopard-skin bow case holds the black arrows of the wind.
His crystal sword is the invincible wisdom of spontaneous liberation.
With his right hand, he raises a terrifying whip
Slashing through all deceptions.
With his left, he raises a victory banner the color of the dawn.
With a saddle and bridle of pure white jade, Kyang Go Karkar,

The power of confidence and wind of winds,
Stands beside his throne, clouds billowing from his nostrils.

All around him the air is filled, like a gathering storm,
With hosts of mounted Drala and Werma warriors.
Their golden armor and steel swordblades flash like lightning.

Above him, in the center of the sky,
The King of the Lha domain, youthful and vibrant,
In crystal armor, rides on his snow-white horse,
While his lustrous pennants and those of his hosts of Drala warriors
Snap in the wind with the sound of cracking glacier ice.

Below him, at the bottom of the world ocean,
The Naga King of the Lu domain, powerful and wise,
In turquoise armor with his sea-blue horse,
Sits in the deep caverns of his jewel palace.
His warriors and emissaries
Move ceaselessly beneath earth and sea.

With a voice soft and penetrating as spring rain, the Lion Lord
then addresses his subjects:

Great Queen, noble lords and ladies,
Loyal and fearless warriors of Ling,
Even though our journey is endless,
Our time together will soon be over.

When I was born, the blessings of the Rigdens
Took indestructible form in this shifting world.
When I won the throne of Ling,

The wisdom of the ancestral sovereigns
Was fulfilled in this world as authentic presence.

When I opened the treasury of Magyel Pomra,
The display of enriching presence
Provided the weapons to overcome aggression and fear.

When I conquered the Tirthikas,
The belief in an external savior was cut through
By the primordial stroke of Ashe.

This is the great stroke,
Drawn with the heart's blood of the Rigdens,
That conquers all the demon realms.
It unifies the hidden kingdom of the human heart,
And sets free the accomplishment of the four dignities.

So from the conquest of Lutzen, black demon of fearful death,
Arose the Lion warriorship of unconditioned delight.
So from the conquest of the Hor demons of defilement,
Arose the Tiger warriorship of vast inquisitive confidence.
So from the conquest of Jang, the red demon realm of godlike
     desire,
Arose the Garuda warriorship beyond the conventions of hope
     and fear.
So from the conquest of Shingti, the yellow demon of raw
     accumulation,
Arose the Dragon warriorship of action that does not require
     confirmation.

Now because we have taken this journey together
As one heart and one mind,

The vision of the Great Eastern Sun
Has dawned in this world.
The path of spirituality and a worldly life
Are inseparable in warriorship.

Now, from my heart, I give this to you.
It is the heart of the warrior and it is yours.

Then the Lion Lord, Gesar, King of Ling, seated as an Imperial Rigden on the throne of the Great Nyen, draws himself up, and it seems that his head touches the sky and his shoulders are immense and powerful as a mountain range. From a syllable in Gesar's heart emerges the great stroke, drawn from the ink of the Rigdens' heart blood. It radiates from his heart and enters the foreheads of Queen Sechan Dugmo and all the lords, ladies and warriors of Ling. Slowly it descends into their hearts where, pulsing and vibrating, it remains. Gesar and his subjects are one in this view, meditation and action. Then the Lion Lord sings a song of a warrior's joy:

Entering decisively into relative reality
Is the direct experience of basic goodness.
Committing our lives to the father Dralas,
Is the direct experience of the Great Eastern Sun.
Committing ourselves to the Imperial Rigdens,
Is the direct experience of Shambhala dignity.
Committing ourselves to the Mother lineage of Dralas,
Is the direct experience of elegance and mercy.
Destroying the enemies that steal away the human mind,
Is the direct experience of unconditional confidence.
Leaping beyond the limits of aggression,

Is the direct experience of the Kingdom of Shambhala.

This is the heart of all the Rigden Fathers.
This is the essence of warriorship.
This is the heart of all mankind.
This is the absolute nonduality of *kaya* and *jnana*,
The nonduality of space and awareness,
The heartbeat of the world.
This is our truth, aspiration and vow.

And so they sit in meditation for three years, sustaining and sustained by unwavering confidence. To some travelers or herdsmen who chance to see them, they appear as a vision, unforgettably splendid and immutable; to others, they appear simply as a bright light on the mountainside; to others a faint glow; and to some, though they feel unaccountably happy as they pass by this mountain, Gesar and his warriors are completely invisible.

3

At the end of the allotted time, the Lion Lord rouses his followers. It is a warm day in late autumn, and the air is filled with the diffuse golden light of a waning sun. Gesar sings to them this song of completion:

This is the completion of our time together.
Hesitation, depression, fear and doubt are ended.
Nothing has power over you.
All that is innate in goodness is yours.
Your feet are yours again.

Your legs are yours again.
Your body is yours again.
Your voice is yours again.
Your words are yours again.
Your perception is yours again.
What you perceive is yours again.
Your mind is yours again.
What you are aware of is yours again.
Your power of movement is yours again.
Your power to live is yours again.
This is the offering of basic goodness.
Guard it and use it.
Do not forget it when darkness comes again to this world.
Whatever happens in your life is worthy of being your path.

4

The nobles, great ladies, warriors and people of Ling depart quietly and return to their homes, while Sechan Dugmo, Kyang Go Karkar and a few attendants remain behind. The silent caravan of the subjects of Ling comes to a halt as it reaches a crest across the valley from where Gesar and his retinue sit, and they turn to take a last distant look at their sovereign. It is like looking at the last rays of sunset, glowing on a distant mountain peak. Expressing all their feelings, it is Todong's son who sings this song of gratitude and parting:

The wounded mind,
Battered from searching for completion

In unsettled dreams of meeting and parting,
Is now spontaneously restored
In seeing the crystal light of AH,
The undivided clarity of Rigpa.

The wounded mind,
Cut, seeking to fulfill existence
In the razor coils of time,
Is spontaneously restored
In the life of the crystal light of AH,
The seamless continuity of the Great Eastern Sun.

The wounded mind,
Wavering and dazed from gazing
In the mirror of alien projections,
Is spontaneously restored
In resting in the crystal light of AH,
The undivided simplicity of space.

Because what is called oneself and the world
Cannot be split,
Mind is spontaneously restored
From the throbbing ache of continual bewilderment,
By surrendering in the dazzling ocean,
The infinite qualities of the crystal light of AH.

Because ignorance is not the root of mind,
And no teacher teaches and no student follows,
All the surly bitter wounds of doubt
Are spontaneously resolved
In the vibrant reality of Gesar's blessing,
The complete action of the crystal light of AH.

Because mind rests only in itself,
The self-existing light of luminous omniscience,
Inseparable from the name of our only father, Gesar,
Cannot diminish or fail,
Even amid painful illusions of life and death.
The first and the last moments are the same.

As Todong's son sings this song, the people of Ling perform the solemn dance called, "The Cycle Appears At Completion," and when it is done, the people of Ling return to their homes. At sunrise the next morning, Gesar and his companions go to a large cave on the face of the white mountain, which looks out over a landscape of rivers and valleys and across them to range upon range of snow-capped mountains. This cave was once the retreat place of Padma Sambhava, and on the black rock wall at its rear is the mark of absolute Ashe. By evening, they have settled there.

5

As night falls, a radiant full moon rises in the clear black sky, and by its light, the world around them becomes bright, still, mysterious and poignant. As Kyang Go Karkar stands quietly by the door, they all sit in a circle at the center of the cavern. Gesar's voice is steady and clear:

Now that our work is done,
There is no need for these bodies to perpetuate themselves.
The truth of confidence and wakefulness
Does not depend on the appearances of existence,
And is not threatened by the delusions of nonexistence.
The body, as is said, is an object on loan,

And now it is time that its constituents return to their own nature.

Let earth return to the mountains and plains of this world.
Let water return to rivers, lakes and seas.
Let heat return to the flames of hearth and camp fire.
Let wind return to the air of this sky.
Let the elements of red and white
Return as the blessings of sun and moon
In the pure sky of the avadhuti.

In this way, may our existence,
Impartial in its love, unbiased in its brilliance,
Bless, guide and protect
All who dwell in this world for as long as it remains.

With this vow, Gesar and his heart companions sit motionless throughout the night. When the first sunbeam of dawn shoots an arrow of light above the distant mountains, then with a great roar of confidence they shout the great warrior syllables, and in the cave on the face of the white mountain, there remain only empty clothes and a faint rainbow of light.

That morning, as day is about to break, a giant rainbow circles the Kingdom of Ling. Framed by this vivid rainbow, the sun and moon both shine, and stars are sparkling in the pink sky of a windy dawn. For three days, nothing in the sky moves.

6

In that time and thereafter, when the people of Ling look at the sun, Gesar is present; when they look at the moon, Sechan

Dugmo is present. In the stars, all who have ever aided the Lion Lord are present, and in the winds, they feel that they themselves are riding his wonder horse, Kyang Go Karkar. As they live through the cycles of the years, they celebrate and make offerings as the seasons change. Living in harmony amongst themselves and with the world, the Kingdom of Ling remains powerful. They uphold the sacred way of warriorship and train their children in its disciplines. Thus they are never separate from the life force of the Lion Lord.

So, now and hereafter, by calling on the name of Gesar, Lion King of Ling, by singing his songs and recounting his deeds, by invoking his inspiration and heroic discipline, by making these offerings to him, may the confidence and power of goodness remain in this world, inseparable in our hearts from the being of the profound, brilliant, just, powerful, all-victorious one, the supreme protector of this earth.

KI KI SO SO ASHE SAMAYA JHA
TAK SENG KYUNG DRUK DI YAR KYE

COLOPHON

This has been set down drawing on the profound and vast mind ocean of the incomparable one, Chokyi Gyatso, the eleventh Trungpa Tulku, the Druk Sakyong, the Dorje Dradul of Mukpo Dong.

Just as a traveler, seeing an immense and beautiful lake from afar, may still make a sketch that gives a slight impression of it, just so, at the request of my dear friend Gendun Nyima, with the encouragement of my life-long friend Zopa Detso, and with the thought of my son, Orgyen Chophel Jigme Dorje, ever in my heart, I have written this.

This is dedicated to the longevity and fulfillment of all the wishes of Sakyong Mipham Jampal Trinlay Dradul. May all the aspirations of the Shambhala Lineage, without a single exception, be swiftly and completely accomplished.

So, as the Dorje Dradul himself has written:

By the confidence of the Golden Sun of the Great East,
May the lotus garden of the Rigden's wisdom bloom.
May the dark ignorance of sentient beings be dispelled.
May all beings enjoy profound brilliant glory.

May this be so.

Douglas J. Penick,
Chodzin Paden,
Magyel Pomra Sayi Dakpo
Los Angeles, CA

TEXTUAL ACKNOWLEDGEMENTS

This text contains echoes, paraphrases, and borrowings from the following:

(1) The entire works of Chögyam Trungpa Rinpoche.

(2) *The Superhuman Life of Gesar of Ling.* Alexandra David-Neel. Boston: Prajna Press, 1981. In particular, there is a paraphrase on pp. 29–31 from her rendition of the text from pp. 117–119.

(3) *Gessar Khan.* Ida Zeitlin. New York: G. H. Doran & Co., 1927.

(4) *The Religions of Mongolia.* Walther Hessig. London: Routledge and Kegan Paul, Ltd., 1980.

(5) Notes taken by Robert Newman of talks given by Yangthang Tulku in New York in 1991.

(6) *The Myths and Prayers of The Great Star Chant.* Wheelwright and McAllester. Tsaile, Arizona: Navajo Community College Press, 1988. Paraphrase on p. 105 is from p. 88.

NOTES TO THE INTRODUCTION

1. *dGra 'Dul Nor Bu'i sNying Thig* (GNN) by Mipham Namgyal (1846–1912), from *The Writings of 'Jam Mgon Mi Pham Rgya mTsho* (Lama Ngodrup and Sherap Drimey, India), vol. *Na,* p. 26B/3.

2. Ling was the name of a country. Gesar means Blossom Pistil, or, as R.A. Stein writes in his introduction for *Dzam Gling Ge Sar rGyal Po'i rTogs brJod, The Epics of Gesar* (EG), (Kunzang Topgyel, Bhutan), vol. I, p. 19: "Gesar is a transcription of the, first Greek, and later Turkish, title *kaisar* ("king" or "emperor")." If so, after conquering some Persian and/or some Turkish tribes, Gesar could have received the title in the same way that the third Dalai Lama was offered the title of 'Dalai Lama' by Altan Khan, a Mongol king.

3. The dates of Gesar's life are uncertain. Some believe that he lived in the eleventh century and others in the thirteenth: *bsTan rTris Kun Las bTus Pa* by Tseten Zhabtrung (1910– ?) (mTsho sNgon Mi Rigs dPe bsKrun Khang, China), p. 152: "Lingje Gesar was born in the iron-rat year (A.D. 1000)." Lingje means the Lord of Ling. And p. 165: "According to the prophecies of rLang Byang Ch'ub 'Dre

Khol, Gesar died at the age of 88, in the fire-hare year of the second Rabjung, 1087."

Deb Ther rGya mTsho (DG) by Trag-gon Zhabtrung Konchog Tenpa Rabgye (1801– ?) (India), vol. I, p. 562/13: Gesar was born either in the iron-rat (1060) or in the water-snake year (1053) of the first Rabjung. Gesar received teachings from Lang Drekol and Smritijnanakirti (tenth–eleventh centuries).

The Nyingma School of Tibetan Buddhism (NSTB) by Dudjom Rinpoche (1904–1987) (Wisdom Publications), vol. I, p. 952: "Lingje Gesar, born in the earth-tiger year (1038) was in his fiftieth year, when the second Rabjung began (1027)."

Bod Kyi Lo rGyus (rGyal Rabs) by Dudjom Rinpoche (Dupjung Lama, India), p. 187b/6: "Lingje Gesar seems to have lived during the time of Ngadag Palkhor Tsen (924–954) and his sons."

EG, vol. I, "Gleng brJod (Introduction) by Penala," p. 10/2: "[Gesar] was born in A.D. 1038 in the earth-male tiger year of the first Rabjung cycle."

Bod Kyi Srid Don rGyal Rabs (BSG) by W.D. Shakabpa (1907– ?) (Tsepal Taikhang, India), vol. I, p. 256–261: A friend of Shakabpa's told him, "Kathog Situ and Jamgon Khyentse have said that Drogon Chögyal Phagpa (1235–1280) couldn't go by the northern route on his second trip to China (1267) because of the war between Ling and Hor." However, Shakabpa adds that he couldn't find this story in any Sakya sources.

My teacher, Kyala Khenpo (1893–1957), told me, "Chögyal Phagpa couldn't travel to China by way of Amdo because of the war between Ling and the Mongols, and he turned south. On the way he was received at Tsangchen field of

Do Valley by 500 monks of Deur Chöje Monastery." Today, in Tsangchen field of Do Valley stands the Dodrupchen Monastery, but it is true that Deur Chöje, a Sakyapa monastery, was situated there, and the ruins are still visible. However, it is not certain that Chögyal Phagpa ever traveled here or, if he did, why.

rLang Gi Po Ti bSe Ru (LPS) by rLang Byang Ch'ub 'Dre Khol (Bod Rang sKyong lJongs, Tibet), p. 46–49: It says, rLang 'Dre Khol visited Gesar and Ling twice, subdued the demonic forces of the four directions and gave teachings and blessings. LPS was written at the time of Gesar, and this is the earliest literature that mentions Gesar of Ling, but the time of rLang 'Dre Khol himself is in question.

Ch'os 'Bying mKhas Pa dGa' Byed by Guru Trashi (nineteenth century) (Grung Go'i Bod Kyi Shes Rig dPe bsKrun Khang, China), p. 170 and *Rin Ch'en Baidurya'i Phreng Ba* (gTer rNam) by Kongtul Yonten Gyatso (1813–1903) (Jamyang Khyentse, India), folio 22b/4, say that rLang 'Dre Khol was the father of rLang dPal Gyi Seng Ge, one of the twenty-five main disciples of Guru Rinpoche. *Bod Kyi Deb Ther dPyid Kyi rGyal Mo'i Glu dByangs* by the Fifth Dalai Lama (1617–1682) (Mi Rigs dPe bsKrun Khang, China), p. 1223/4, mentions a dPal Gyi Seng Ge as being a son of rLang 'Dre Khol, though he is not clear whether he was a disciple of Guru Rinpoche.

Bur rLang 'Dre Khol must have come after rLang dPal Gyi Seng Ge, the one who was a disciple of Guru Rinpoche, as LPS, p. 40 mentions that Guru Rinpoche gave prophecies to rLang dPal Gyi Seng Ge concerning rLang 'Dre Khol's coming in the Lang clan in the future, and LPS, p. 2/14 also says that there were two masters named dPal Gyi Seng Ge and thirteen masters named

Byang Ch'ub in the rLang clan. Also Gesar came much later than Guru Rinpoche.

Bibliographical Dictionary of Tibet and Tibetan Buddhism by Khetsun Sangpo (Library of Tibetan Works and Archives, Dharamsala, India), vol. IV, p. 97–98: "As [DG and NSTB] agreed, Gesar appeared in the first Rabjung. NSTB says that he was born in the earth-tiger year (1038), and LPSG writes that he lived for 88 years. So he must have been killed in the wood-dragon year (1124) by 'Dan Ma, as *Zhal lChe bChu Drug* writes: 'King Gesar of the lower (province) was killed by Denma. But the blood-money has still not been paid.'"

However, throughout Drung literature, there is no report that Gesar of Ling was killed, let alone by Denma, one of his chief commanders.

4. Although some texts on Gesar indicate that Gesar was born in Ma Valley, the majority of the sources seem to agree that Gesar was born at Kyid Sos Yag Gi Kha mDo in Dza Valley. At the age seven or eight, he moved to Ma Valley where he then settled.

DG, vol. I, p. 562/20: "There are different views. Some say Gesar was born at mTsho Gor Kha by the Dza river near Tshab Tsha Monastery, while others say that he was born at Dar [Gyi] Sa Nag Lung of Dar gorge (of Ma Valley). These are now inhabited mostly by Golok people."

Heart of Asia by Nicholas Roerich (1874–1947) (Inner Traditions International), p. 102/25: "Ladakh is regarded as the birthplace of Gesar Khan." Although this view is improbable, it shows that many places claim having given birth to Gesar.

5. Some sources say that Gesar's father was a divine presence, and not the human being Singlen.

6. *The Monguors of Kansu-Tibetan Frontier* by Louis M. J. Schram (The American Philosophical Society, 1954), p. 24(b)/48: "Potanin notes a tradition according to which the Shirongols had built a large realm, the capital of which was Lanchou (capital of the province of Kansu); after three mighty emperors governed the realm in succession it was destroyed by Gesar (the mythical Tibetan hero)." Were the Gurkar (Kerker?) of Hor and the Shirongol the same? The Shirongol (or Mongour) was a tribal group originally from Mongolia that settled in Kansu province.

7. *Oracles and Demons of Tibet* by Rene de Nebesky-Wojkowitz (Akademische Druk-u. Verglagsanstalt, Graz/ Austria, 1975), p. 101, and some other Western sources say that Pehar, the chief Dharmapala of Samye Monastery, was subdued by Gesar and so on. But Pehar was subdued and converted as a Dharmapala by Guru Rinpoche in the ninth century A.D. Gesar of Ling is different from Gesar Mag, a country mentioned in the chronicles of the Chögyal Dynasty.

8. *Ne Shar Lo rGyus Jo Glang Gangs A'od* by Sangye Tendzin, p. 6: The Sharpas of Nepal originally came from Kham. They fled to Nepal through central Tibet because of the upheavals caused by the wars of Ling.

9. The late king of Lingtsang [quoted earlier] told me: "My family lineage is derived from Dralha Tsegyal, and the library of my palace had the list of all my forefathers, from Dralha to myself." Dralha Tsegyal was the son of Gyatsa Zhalkar, the

half brother of Gesar.

10. LPS, pp. 45–74 and 84–86 and other sources state: rLang Byang Ch'ub 'Dre bKol visited Ling many times and became the teacher of Gesar. He died at the age of 108.

11. *Sog Li Tri rTa rDzong* by Drungter Nyima Rangshar (Si Khron Mi Rigs dPe bsKrun Khang), p. 218.

12. Besides the events of Gesar mentioned in LPS, one of the earliest known surviving writings on Gesar may be a ritual text that was written in Mongolian in A.D. 1600. See introduction to EG by R. A. Stein.

13. *Ri Bo Himala'i bsTan bChos* by Gedun Chöphel (1905–1951) (Si Khron Mi Rigs dPe bsKrun Khang, China), p. 350/7.

14. For further explanation regarding Mind Ter, see *Hidden Teachings of Tibet* by Tulku Thondup Rinpoche. Boston: Wisdom Publications, 1986.

15. *gSer Ch'os A'og Min bGrod Pa'i Them sKas* by Tragthung Dorje (Do Khyentse, 1800–1866) (Si Khron Mi Rigs dPe bsKrun Khang, China). p. 56/10.

16. GNN, p. 26B/3.

17. NSTB, vol. I, p. 960/3 and others.

GLOSSARY

amrita: (Lit. deathless). Elixir which sustains beyond death; spiritual intoxication.

Ashe: (Lit. primordial stroke). The stroke which cuts through all aggression toward self and other and draws forth the primordial human dignity.

Drala: (Lit. above enemy). The transcendent and worldly power that exists spontaneously in the direct perception of phenomena. The worldly Dralas are the specific communicative nature of sky, mountain, earth, water and below the earth.

Four-Armed Mahakala: (Lit. great black one). A principal wrathful protector of the Buddhist teachings who guards both the teachings and the practitioner.

Great Eastern Sun: Ever-present, pure, nurturing radiance which is the primordial source of human confidence.

gzhi: A form of black- and white-banded agate unique to Tibet.

jnana: Wisdom, or primordial presence.

kaya: Body or form as in the three bodies (or forms) of the Buddha: Dharmakaya (body of truth); Sambhogakaya (body of enjoyment); and Nirmanakaya (emanation body as manifest in physical form).

KI *and* SO: Syllables in the warrior cry which brings down the power of Werma and Drala.

Lha, Nyen, Lu: The natural hierarchy of, high, middle and low, respectively. These terms refer as well to the Dralas of each.

Magyel Pomra: Dharma protector and Drala associated with Mount Amnye Machen in Golok, which is sometimes called by that name.

Padma Sambhava: The great Indian teacher considered to be the second Buddha, who brought Vajrayana Buddhism to Tibet in the eighth century.

Rigden: The title of the rulers of the Kingdom of Shambhala.

torma: A ritual offering cake.

Werma: The lineages of ancestral warrior protectors. Sometimes synonymous with Drala, and sometimes refers to their retinue.

Windhorse: The primordial energy of basic goodness and of human existence.

Vajra Kilaya: The action aspect of the Buddha and wrathful aspect of Vajrasattva, which overcome all inner and outer obstacles.

ABOUT THE AUTHOR

Douglas J. Penick was born in 1944, graduated from Princeton University, and has studied with the Vidyadhara, the Venerable Chögyam Trungpa Rinpoche since 1971. He lives in Boulder, Colorado.

He is the author of several novels, plays, and many short stories and poems. His work has appeared in periodicals in the U.S., Canada, and France. He also wrote the English language version of the National Film Board of Canada/NHK documentary, *The Tibetan Book of the Dead.*

Mr. Penick's work in collaboration with the composer Peter Lieberson include *Five Songs*; *King Gesar*, whose text is derived from this book and which will be released on Sony CD this fall; and *Ashoka's Dream*, which will premiere at the Santa Fe Opera in the summer of 1997.

WISDOM PUBLICATIONS

WISDOM PUBLICATIONS is a non-profit publisher of books on Buddhism, Tibet, and related East-West themes. We publish our titles with the appreciation of Buddhism as a living philosophy and the special commitment of preserving and transmitting important works from all the major Buddhist traditions.

If you would like more information, a copy of our mail order catalogue, or to be kept informed about our future publications, please write or call us at:

361 Newbury Street
Boston, Massachusetts 02115
USA
Telephone: (617) 536-3358
Fax: (617) 536-1897

THE WISDOM TRUST

As a non-profit publisher, Wisdom is dedicated to the publication of fine Dharma books for the benefit of all sentient beings. We depend upon sponsors in order to publish books like the one you are holding in your hand.

If you would like to make a donation to the Wisdom Trust Fund to help us continue our Dharma work, or to receive information about opportunities for planned giving, please write to our Boston office.

Thank you so much.

Wisdom Publications is a non-profit, charitable 501(c)(3) organization and a part of the Foundation for the Preservation of the Mahayana Tradition (FPMT).

CARE OF DHARMA BOOKS

DHARMA BOOKS CONTAIN THE TEACHINGS of the Buddha; they have the power to protect against lower rebirth and to point the way to liberation. Therefore, they should be treated with respect—kept off the floor and places where people sit or walk—and not stepped over. They should be covered or protected for transporting and kept in a high, clean place separate from more "mundane" materials. Other objects should not be placed on top of Dharma books and materials. Licking the fingers to turn pages is considered bad form (and negative karma). If it is necessary to dispose of Dharma materials, they should be burned with care and awareness rather than thrown in the trash. When burning Dharma texts, it is considered skillful to first recite a prayer or mantra, such as OM, AH, HUNG. Then, you can visualize the letters of the texts (to be burned) absorbing into the AH, and the AH absorbing into you. After that, you can burn the texts.

These considerations may also be kept in mind for Dharma artwork, as well as the written teachings and artwork of other religions.

DRINKING THE MOUNTAIN STREAM
Songs of Tibet's Beloved Saint, Milarepa
Translated by Lama Kunga Rinpoche and Brian Cutillo

Milarepa, Tibet's renowned and beloved saint, wandered the terrain of eleventh-century Tibet guiding countless followers along the Buddhist path through his songs of realization. Milarepa's songs and poems are bold and inspiring, his language direct and immediate. Lama Kunga Rinpoche and Brian Cutillo render a faithful translation of this rare collection of Milarepa's songs.

$14.95, 192 pages, 0-86171-063-0

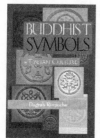

BUDDHIST SYMBOLS IN TIBETAN CULTURE
Dagyab Rinpoche
Foreword by Robert A.F. Thurman

The Queen's Earrings. The Fur-Bearing Fish. The Endless Knot. Tibetan Buddhism is filled with rich, colorful symbols. But what do they all mean? In this fascinating study, Dagyab Rinpoche presents the nine-best known groups of Tibetan Buddhist symbols, tracing their evolution through Tibetan and Indian rituals and sacred texts.

"Symbolism is the language of the human spirit, and this book is the most systematic study of its Tibetan idiom that has yet appeared."—Huston Smith, author of *The Illustrated World's Religions*

"The author deserves our thanks.... Highly recommended."—Herbert Guenther, author of *Wholeness Lost and Wholeness Regained*

$14.95, 160 pages, 0-86171-047-9